GENTLE ANNIE

The True Story of a Civil War Nurse

GENTLE ANNIE

The True Story of a Civil War Nurse

MARY FRANCIS SHURA

SCHOLASTIC
HARDCOVER

Scholastic Inc.
New York

Library of Congress Cataloging-in-Publication Data

Shura, Mary Francis, 1923–
Gentle Annie:
the true story of a civil war nurse / Mary Francis Shura.
p. cm.
Summary: A biography of Anna Blair Etheridge, a nurse during the
Civil War, from childhood through her four years of service with the
Army of the Potomac.
ISBN 0-590-44367-4

1. Etheridge, Anna Blair — Juvenile literature. 2. United States —
History — Civil War, 1861–1865 — Medical care — Juvenile litera-
ture. 3. Nurses — United States — Biography — Juvenile literature.
[1. Etheridge, Anna Blair. 2. Nurses. 3. United States — History —
Civil War, 1861–1865.] I. Title.
E621.E78S58 1991
973.7'75'092 — dc20
[B]
[92]
90-39251
CIP
AC

12 11 10 9 8 7 6 5 4 3 2 1   1 2 3 4 5 6/9

Printed in the U.S.A.   37

First Scholastic printing, February 1991

Acknowledgments

Writers intent on walking honestly backward in time start their journeys through the doors of the library. Once there, they are dependent on the skill and patience of those custodians of the past known as librarians.

Space prohibits my listing all the priceless people involved, but I must offer my gratitude and appreciation for the interest and cooperation I received from the following:

Burton Historical Collection, Detroit Public Library, Detroit, Michigan

Indian Prairie Library, Darien, Illinois, as well as the impressive resources of the Suburban Library System

Newberry Library, Chicago, Illinois

New York Academy of Medicine Library, New York, New York

Also my warm thanks to John Dobberton, Ed and Dixie Otto, and Craig Pugh for invaluable support and assistance.

One

Detroit, Michigan
May 3, 1854

WHEN ANNIE HEARD the pony cart stop out front, she ran to her window. Mrs. Hammer had *actually* let Sophie drive the pony cart over to Annie's house. When Sophie hadn't come right after lunch, Annie was sure her mother hadn't given her permission. Mrs. Hammer acted as if girls were made of spun sugar, but she let Sophie's pesky brother, Will, do anything he wanted to.

Although she could hardly see the pony trap or who was driving it, Annie leaned on the sill to call out to Sophie.

Then she gasped. It wasn't Sophie but Will who was driving. He was the last person on earth Annie wanted to see on her birthday. Will thought himself special just because he was older

1

and a boy. He sneered at her and Sophie and made dreadful fun of them. Annie pulled back as Will jumped out of the cart.

Annie heard the housekeeper, Belle, going to the front door. She didn't have to go down. Just let Will give his message to Belle and trot right back home!

If Sophie wasn't coming, Annie's birthday was ruined. Sophie *always* came on Annie's birthday afternoon. Belle, who had taken care of Annie and her father since Annie's mother died of cholera, baked a special cake. Then Annie and Sophie got to play from right after lunch until almost supper.

They used to have doll tea parties. That was too babyish now that they were ten. Annie had thought up a marvelous adventure. Now Will had to come and spoil everything!

When Belle called from the hall below, Annie didn't answer. Could Sophie have told her mother that they planned to drive the pony cart around the park the way the older girls drove their buggies?

Belle called again with a hint of warning in her tone. Annie made a face but dragged slowly down the stairs. What did she have to say to any old twelve-year-old boy, much less Will Hammer?

She stopped on the next to the bottom step. Will sure didn't look happy. He was stirring from one foot to the other, twisting his hat in his hands.

Belle turned to her. "Master Will has a message for you," Belle said. Belle looked confused as if she didn't understand what was going on either.

Will spoke up fiercely. "My sister wishes you a happy birthday and is sorry that she can't join you this afternoon." He practically spit the words out and looked ready to turn and bolt out of the door the minute he was through.

Belle frowned with sympathy. "Poor dear Sophie," she said. "I hope she's not sick."

"Not really," he stammered, his tone not quite so angry. "Not what you'd call sick sick."

At Belle's puzzled look, Will grumbled, "Just a fit, that's all."

Annie swallowed her giggles at Belle's startled look.

"Well, Miss Annie would be honored if *you* would stay and enjoy some of her birthday cake," Belle said. "Then we could send a slice home with you for poor dear Sophie."

Annie groaned inside. If Will accepted, Annie would have to be polite to him because Belle would be watching.

Will moistened his lips with his tongue, clearly remembering how good Belle's cakes were.

Belle smiled. "Oh, come on, Will. You'll be sorry if you don't."

He hesitated only a moment, then put his cap in Belle's outstretched hand. As soon as the kitchen door closed behind her, Annie could finally giggle.

"What's so funny?" Will asked, glaring at her. "I didn't want to come here any more than you want me here."

Annie shook her head. "I wasn't laughing at you. Didn't you see how surprised Belle was when you said the word *fit*? She thinks only *terribly* sick people have fits. She's never seen one of Sophie's temper tantrums."

Will chuckled, then grinned. "Lucky Belle."

"You might as well sit down," Annie told him, perching on a chair by the fireplace. "What was *this* fit about?"

He shrugged, "A hat with a feather. She wanted to wear her Sunday dress and hat and kicked up a fuss when Mother wouldn't let her." He paused, shaking his head. "I don't get it. Why did she want to get dressed up just to come play?"

"It's my birthday," Annie told him.

"She wore regular clothes on your other birthdays," he reminded her. His dark eyes narrowed. "What were you up to?"

When Annie shrugged, he shook his head. "I know that look, Annie. What crazy bee did you put in my sister's bonnet this time?"

"How do you know it was my idea?" she asked.

" 'Cause Sophie's afraid of her shadow, and you're always trying new things."

Since he didn't sound cross but only amused, Annie laughed. "We were going to drive around the park in the pony cart," she admitted.

He almost jumped out of his seat. "Just the two of you? You know Mother would never let Sophie do that. I'm only allowed because I'm older and a boy. But you little kids?"

Annie would have reminded him that she was ten whole years old but the door swung open. Belle wheeled in the tea cart with ice tinkling musically in a tall pitcher of lemonade. Will jumped to his feet and whistled softly at the tall golden cake on the crystal cake stand.

"Butterscotch," Belle said with just a hint of pride. "Four layers, with pecan filling." She cut them both a generous slice, filled two tumblers, and stood looking at them with satisfaction. "I'll be in the kitchen if you need anything," she said after a minute.

Annie cut Will's second slice and just a little wedge more for herself. Will didn't look cross anymore, but full and a little sticky around his mouth. "I could take you riding in the park if you'd like," he said. "Just because it's your birthday and all."

"You don't have to do that," she said.

"I know it," he said, licking the icing off his upper lip. "Only you have to promise not to squeal if I go fast."

"I never squeal," Annie told him.

"How would I know that?" he asked. "Sophie does enough of it for both of you. If you want to, I'll ask Miss Belle."

Annie smiled. "I'd love it," she admitted. "I really would."

Belle said what she always said. "I wish I knew what Annie's father would say." She never did know because he was never there. He left in the dark of the morning for his store downtown and came back after the street lamps had been lit. "You will be extra careful?" she asked Will.

He nodded so solemnly that she was convinced. Annie shot out the front door fast before Belle got time to have a second thought.

Annie realized that riding with Will was more fun than it would have been with Sophie. Will *did* drive fast, so fast that she had to hang onto her bonnet and the side of the cart. At the first turn she laughed out loud. The second time around he handed her the reins and told her she could drive.

The pony picked up his heels to a wonderful rollicking clip. "Hey, Annie," Will cried, hanging on as hard as she had.

When Annie saw the cart ahead of them with

a couple of boys in it, she slapped the reins against the pony's back and whirled past them in a cloud of dust.

"Whatcha think you're doing?" one of the boys yelled.

The other one shouted, "And that's a girl!"

Annie heard the driver yell at his pony and she grinned over at Will. "I don't think he can pass us, do you?"

Will laughed. "No way! But let me drive. It's my turn anyway."

The walkers in the park stopped to watch the race, egging them on. A woman rider who had to dance her bay mare out of the way shouted a lecture to them.

Only twice did the other cart even come close to passing. "Who do you think you are?" the driver shouted.

Will said, "Let's lose them, Annie."

It wasn't hard to do. The other cart was drawn by a fat-bellied pony who was getting winded. When Will turned the cart out of the park and started down the street, the boys were still back under the trees, shouting and waving their fists.

"Good show, Annie," Will said. "What made you think of that?"

She shrugged. "I just like excitement, I guess."

Back at the house, Belle had fixed a tray of cake for the Hammer family. "Give Miss Sophie our love and tell her to get well fast," she told

Will. Then she smiled at him the way she did when she was close to tears. "What a little gentleman you are, Will Hammer, to give our Annie such a lovely birthday ride."

Annie didn't dare look at Will. She knew he was having as much trouble keeping a straight face as she was.

Because she was ten and it was her birthday, Annie's father came home early. As usual, he had the latest newspaper tucked under his arm. Usually he sat with Annie and read the paper with her while Belle finished up dinner. Instead, this night he pulled Annie up on his lap and smiled at her. "Now this is what I call a *special* day."

She looked over at the paper. "Oh," she said. "Was there something exciting in the news? Is there more news from Japan?"

He laughed and held her close. "That's my girl. Mine must be the only little girl in Detroit who even *knows* about Commodore Perry's excursion to open trade with Japan."

"You always say it's my world, too," she reminded him.

"It is," he nodded. "And it makes me happy that you like to keep track of it the way I do. But this day is special because it's your birthday. Was it a good one?"

"Better than that. It was wonderful," she said. "I even made a new friend."

"That *is* wonderful," he agreed, his face turning sad.

As his smile faded, Annie was startled to notice how tired he looked, how gray his hair was becoming. She had meant to tell him her new friend was Will, but she only wound her arms around his neck and held him tight.

Then he spoke quietly. "I love you for yourself, Annie. But I love you doubly for how like your mother you are. Along with courage and a gentle spirit, her gift for friendship was more precious than diamonds."

Two

Detroit, Michigan
Summer 1854

ANNIE DIDN'T TELL Belle, but she started noticing strange things. Her father worked longer hours and looked tired and discouraged when he came home. He had talked about the news to her all her life, saying that women needed to be as involved in the world as men were. Now he sometimes didn't even bring a paper home.

Belle was changed, too. She didn't sing or hum around the house. Instead of joints of beef, she served stews with lots of carrots and little potatoes. She quit baking cakes that took a dozen eggs and a bowl of sweet butter.

The mystery didn't keep Annie from having a fun summer with Will. Sophie squealed and protested and hung back a lot. But Annie loved

10

it. Will wasn't afraid of anything. Except for that nagging worry in the back of her mind, it was the jolliest summer Annie could ever remember.

The fun ended suddenly. One August afternoon Annie's father came home early and pulled her onto his lap.

"I have hard news for you, Annie. We're going to move."

"Move!" she cried, twisting to look up at his face.

He shook his head. "Please don't interrupt. I don't like this any better than you do. But this has been a year of reverses. We have to sell out, Annie. Everything."

She stared at him. Everything? He couldn't mean the house and stable and carriage and horses. He couldn't mean her mother's fine furniture and Turkish rugs. He *couldn't* mean her bedroom things — her oval mirror and brass bed.

"But where will we live?" she asked, trying to keep her sudden tears out of her voice.

"Wisconsin. I have a position in Milwaukee working for another merchant. We'll rent a house and start all over, you and I."

"And Belle," she said.

He shook his head. "Not Belle. She's getting on in years. Between her savings and what I can spare, she'll be fine. You're a big girl going on eleven and Belle has taught you well. We'll have a good life, the two of us."

11

She didn't know her father could sound pitiful, but suddenly he did. He was almost begging her to understand and not love him less. She hugged him, hiding her face against his coat. "We'll be fine," she echoed. "Just the two of us."

"That's my girl," he said, holding her tight. "You are your sainted mother all over again."

Annie wished she would remember her mother. She knew how beautiful she was from the framed picture over the parlor fireplace. She knew that right after they married, her mother had come west in a covered wagon with Annie's father to make a new life. Most of all, she knew from her father and Belle how brave and gentle and warm-natured she was. Sometimes Annie almost resented her. How much easier it would be not to have *quite* so much to live up to!

Everything happened very fast. Strangers walked through the house and argued about the value of her mother's things. Belle cried until her eyes were red and then said it was just a late summer cold. Sophie had a tantrum that sent her mother off to bed with a cold cloth on her forehead. "You can't leave," Sophie wailed. "I'll write you all the time but you have to promise to come back."

Will rubbed his boot on the rug and scowled. "I guess I can wish you good luck," he said sullenly. "It sure is rotten enough luck for me."

Then after a minute he added. "I guess I'll just have to miss you."

Annie laughed because otherwise she would have cried. She had promised herself no one would see her do that.

Three

Wisconsin
1854 – 1861

IT WAS A GOOD THING Belle *hadn't* come along.
There was no extra room in the Wisconsin house.
The kitchen was only a part of the main room —
with a small bedroom off at the side.

Annie teased her father that the kitchen kept
her "on her toes." Her supplies and pots and
pans were crammed on high shelves along the
walls. Well water came from a pump on the lean-
to back porch and the bathroom was behind the
house in a cluster of giant trees. Annie's father
insisted that she take the one bedroom. He slept
on a cot in the main room.

How had Belle ever kept that big Detroit house
clean? Annie worked all day just keeping the two
rooms neat, washing and ironing, getting to the

market and back, and putting hot food on her father's table. She baked on Saturday just as Belle always had, and that was the busiest day of all. She really *liked* baking bread except that it took so much time.

Just before Belle got into the carriage to travel to her sister's house in Grand Rapids, she had taken Annie's hands. "Listen to me, child," she had whispered. "And don't tell your father I said this. He's not well. He needs doctoring. He won't hear of that, but you can watch out for him. Feed him good and don't make worry for him."

Annie told herself that Belle was just a worrier but she knew better in her heart. Although her father ate well, he kept losing weight. He smiled only when she spoke to him.

He only seemed like his old self when they talked over the news together. While he rejoiced that Perry had opened the ports of Japan, he shook his head over the endless arguments as to whether the territories of Kansas and Nebraska could have legal slavery when they became states. "Any institution that robs men of their freedom is doomed in America," he told her.

It was in her second week that Annie's first caller came swinging through the woods. The genial young woman with rosy cheeks and ginger-colored freckles introduced herself as Mrs. Clara Jenkins. "I'm sorry I was so slow," she said. "I had two little ones sick when you came and couldn't get away from the rest of them until today. But welcome."

She started at Annie thoughtfully. "Why, you're little more than a child yourself!"

Annie flushed. She was doing a woman's work, wasn't she? "Girls come in all sizes," she told Clara.

Clara laughed. "You make a good point." Still smiling, she emptied a pile of vegetables out on Annie's table. "Not much of a welcome gift but they're from our own garden. They'll keep if you don't let them freeze, and they taste mighty good come winter."

"How wonderful!" Annie said, admiring the golden sweet potatoes and green acorn squash. "How can I ever thank you?"

"Just being here," Clara laughed. "My Hiram is a woodcutter and sometimes is gone for weeks. With my horde, I might as well have my feet nailed to that floor. Just seeing your smoke through the trees is warming."

When Annie learned that the "horde" was three tow-headed children under six, she quit feeling so pushed by her own work. Although they spent little time together, Annie also found it "warming" to know Clara was there.

Sophie's first letter came right away. Annie read it a dozen times, missing Sophie painfully with every word.

Sophie's parents were fine and she had a new

dress she loved. She had to lace her corset so tight to wear it that she couldn't eat. Will was even a worse tease than before.

What could Annie write back? She couldn't let Sophie know how hard her life was. She certainly didn't have any new dresses or corsets to tell about. She wrote about the forests that stretched off west and north of the city. They were too dense for a man to ride a horse between the trees. She told Sophie about the great ships that plowed Lake Michigan and stood at anchor in the harbor, their masts as thick as wheat stalks in a field. She mentioned how worried she was about her father, that his color was sallow and he walked slower than she could ever remember.

For Thanksgiving Annie baked Belle's special raisin and cinnamon bread. The day before the celebration, she carried a hot loaf across to Clara and her family. Hiram was there. He greeted Annie and sniffed the air with gusto.

"You do this sort of thing often?" he asked.

"I bake every Saturday but usually just plain bread."

"There's nothing plain about *any* good bread," he corrected her. "Clara tries, but can't get the knack."

"I had a good teacher," Annie told them.

Annie was halfway home when Hiram hailed her and caught up. "I should be ashamed of myself," he told her, wiping his mouth with the back of his hand. "I couldn't wait to dig into that bread so I didn't. Would you consider baking for us? Cash is slow to find but I'd trade you cut wood and fresh eggs for it."

Annie looked at him in wonder. Hiram's words opened a whole new world. She could *help* her father. She could really help. He wasn't strong enough to chop wood. The eggs might even put some meat on his bones. She knew she should probably get his permission, but what if Hiram changed his mind?

"I'd love to," she told him. "Just tell me how much you want and when."

Sophie's letters kept coming through that long bitter winter and the summer that followed. Annie kept herself from complaining in her own letters. Instead, she wrote about Clara and her funny little children. She described the birds that clamored in the dense woods. She never again mentioned her father's steadily failing health or when he began to cough and pace the dark cabin alone every night.

By November her father was too weak to work.

When he took to his bed the week before Christmas, Annie moved him into the little room where it was quieter.

Clara and Hiram spread word of Annie's baking skill all through their church and their circle of friends. Every week brought new customers.

Annie no longer worried about "keeping" the cabin. Instead she kept the oven of the black range filled with fresh loaves of bread every minute she wasn't busy with her father.

Clara's good friend Millie Smithers had taken care of an ailing mother all her life. When Millie came to buy bread, she visited with Annie's father and taught Annie how to nurse him. Annie learned to change her father's bed and bathe his face and arms to lower his fever. She brewed the herb teas that Millie recommended and made rich milk custards that he barely tasted.

Annie glowed with satisfaction when Clara reported Millie's saying that Annie was a "natural nurse, with a real gift of healing."

As her father spent hours staring out into the woods, Annie could *feel* her own heart breaking. As his eyes grew weak, she read him the news of the world he was leaving so painfully. His highest excitement came when she read him articles about the men working against slavery. When John Brown settled in Kansas to fight slavery there, Annie's father rejoiced in a way that made her heart rise with hope.

Three days after Annie's thirteenth birthday, he died. Annie, numb with grief and tired to her very bones, stood in the warmth of Clara's arms. "What will you do, Annie?" Clara asked, helplessly weeping.

Annie didn't know herself.

"You can't stay here all by yourself," Clara told her.

Annie stared at her. "Where else *can* I go?" she asked.

Clara frowned. "There has to be a right place for such a fine girl," she said. "It's a matter of finding it."

Later Annie looked back on those three years with amazement. There always seemed to be a place she was needed. She had lived for a while with a banker's family to help with the children. After she nursed one of them through a fearful bout with diphtheria, the banker sent her as a companion to his elderly uncle who needed a tender and skillful nurse at home.

But Annie had needs of her own aside from her work. Her loneliness didn't fade with time. When Mr. Etheridge, a friend of her employer's, begged her to become his wife, she finally accepted. No happiness came of the marriage. Night after night she slept on a pillow wet with tears, afraid her marriage was failing. When her restless husband left and did not come back, she returned to her old job and buried herself in her work.

Those were good years. It was almost like having her father back when she read the paper to the banker's uncle and talked to him about the news. He resembled her father in his beliefs, too. When, during a presidential debate, Abraham Lincoln stated that this government could not endure permanently half slave and half free, the old man cheered as her father would have done. When he discovered that Annie had been taught to write a clear hand and was good with numbers, he taught her to keep his ledger and help with the household books.

"How clever you are," Clara cried. "You could do anything you wanted with your life." When Annie didn't answer at once, Clara went on. "What do you want, Annie?"

Annie touched her friend's hand. "I don't know, Clara. I honestly don't know. But when it comes along I'll recognize it." Annie thought of her failed marriage with pain and regret. She didn't add that whatever she chose had to be so great a challenge that succeeding at it would restore her faith in herself.

"Since you get a nice room and board with your salary, you have to be saving," Clara said a little enviously.

"Oh, yes," Annie nodded. "I save almost all I make."

"But you never buy clothes or such," Clara said. "What are you saving for?"

"Having money put away can be important," Annie told her, thinking of Belle, whose savings had meant so much to her, and had been such a help when Belle left their household. "I hope to visit my friend Sophie back in Detroit some day. She's invited me in every letter she's written since I left."

In March of 1861, Annie's patient suffered a stroke and died. She grieved deeply for the kindly, wonderful old man.

"I have a friend whose father needs your services," the banker told her. "I'd be happy to give you an introduction."

"I appreciate that," she told her. "Later I may get in touch with you or him." She felt a sudden bubble of excitement that made her want to laugh aloud.

"I ask from friendly concern," he said. "Do you have plans? Somewhere to go?"

She nodded. "Thank you, sir. I plan to spend my seventeenth birthday with my very dearest friends. Then I will look for another position, maybe back home in Detroit."

She hoped her tone was gentle and ladylike. She didn't *feel* gentle or ladylike at all. Instead, she burst with excitement inside. The more she had thought of returning to Detroit, the more excited she became. There she could begin all over again, turning her thoughts to the future instead of brooding over the past.

Four

Detroit, Michigan
April 1861

ANNIE BOUNCED in the hired coach to Detroit like butter in a runaway churn. The same April warmth that had turned the willow trees golden had melted the road into a swamp of grasping mud. Annie gripped her bag in one gloved hand and clung to the seat with the other. She knew that her hair was tumbling out from under her bonnet brim. And she could feel her petticoats inching up under her long dark skirt. Usually she wouldn't have minded being jostled. This time she did. She had to look her best when Sophie met her carriage.

Before she realized it, the coach's wheels rattled cheerfully along the generous wide streets of

Detroit. Annie's heart leapt with excitement. As the carriage shuddered to a jerking stop she saw Sophie and Will standing in the crowd at the curb. Sophie was dimpled with delight and Will waved madly at the sight of Annie at the window. She almost tumbled out of the door in her excitement.

Sophie seized her in a fragrant hug and Will cried out, "Welcome, Annie, welcome home!" Annie's throat was tight with too much happiness to let her words out.

She had forgotten how luxurious the Hammer house was. When she finished her hot bath, Sophie came to perch on a stool and watch her dress her hair. Annie, glancing at her friend's face, smiled happily. How beautiful Sophie was, but how little the years had changed her!

Oh, she looked grown-up now and elegant with her fair gleaming hair in coils instead of braids. Her crinoline held her petticoats out so wide that they hid the stool and Sophie's satin shoes and a good deal of the rug around her. But she chattered gaily, so full of news and giggles that Annie had only to nod to keep the words flowing.

"You *are* beautiful, you know," Sophie said. "That glorious hair and face. I wonder that they let you go away for fear you wouldn't come back."

Annie chuckled to herself. She hadn't really asked anyone. More than anything this difference separated her from Sophie who had always had the shelter of her family.

The ringing of the dinner bell downstairs stopped Sophie halfway through a story. She jumped to her feet and hugged Annie. "How perfectly splendid to have you here," she said. "Let's make a rule that we will only talk of happy, carefree things. There will be *no* scary talk. We'll go to dances and parties and have picnics by the river."

At Annie's puzzled look, Sophie seized her arm. "Come before the gong sounds again. Papa is difficult enough without having the excuse of our coming late to dinner."

"I can't imagine your father being difficult," Annie admitted as they started down the stairs. Indeed, Mr. Hammer had always been her particular favorite. Like her own father, he had never treated her as if she were an empty-headed doll. Knowing she was a reader, he had always talked to her, even asking her opinion on whatever subject came up.

"He's only gotten crabby and dismal since this stupid trouble with the South began," Sophie said. "I am so sick of his talk of Abraham Lincoln and slavery and going to war that I am like to scream. I declare that he's forgotten how to

laugh. I think he *likes* to frighten Mother and me. He keeps saying that if this rebellion in the South forces us into war, our lives will never be the same again."

Annie stared at her. "But, Sophie," she protested. "He's right. If this comes to war — "

"Don't you start, too!" Sophie said. "The men aren't interested in *my* business, why should I be bored by theirs?"

"Because it's our business, too, that's why," Annie said, losing patience with her. "Don't you realize that the Southerners are trying to take Fort Sumter away from us?"

Sophie looked at her in confusion and then laughed. "Listen to you. That's what comes of reading those silly papers. I for one am having nothing to do with it or them."

The Hammer dining room was as beautiful as Annie remembered it, candlelight glistening on polished silver and china, and wonderful food smells from the swinging door of the kitchen. Annie was so warmly welcomed by both of Sophie's parents that she really *did* feel at home at last.

The difference began between the soup and the main course. During a lull of conversation, Annie heard music from outside. The brisk beat of marching music passed through the heavy draperies of the dining room windows.

Will leaned to catch her eye. What a handsome man he had grown into. And how much he resembled Sophie except that his coloring was deeper. He had the same laughing eyes that had failed to conceal his mischief when they were children. He spoke softly. "That's a band passing in the street," he told her. "Detroit is no longer a quiet, peaceful city."

"William, please," his mother broke in. "You'll not spoil our meal with such talk." Her voice trembled with anger. Annie, remembering what great store Mrs. Hammer put in manners, shrunk with embarrassment for Will. If there was anything Mrs. Hammer hated, it was an unpleasant scene! But what could be so distressing about a bunch of musicians?

Before Will could reply, Mr. Hammer rose and beckoned Annie to the window. "More than a meal will be spoiled before this is over. Come, Annie, see the real world."

It was all Annie could do to make herself follow her host to the window. Behind her, she felt Mrs. Hammer's anger and heard Sophie's exasperated sigh. She gasped and forgot her embarrassment as Mr. Hammer pulled back the drapes.

The band music blared louder. The night was alive with torches bobbing along the street. Glints of light shone on the metal throats of brass instruments, and a boy who could not have been more than eight or nine was running to catch up without missing a beat on his drum. People leaned from windows across the way, waving flags and shouting at the marchers. Horses danced and reared along the crowded street, barely missing the excited demonstrators with their hooves.

Annie looked at her host in puzzled astonishment.

"Patriots," he told her. "Day and night they leave their homes to demonstrate against those traitors in the South. The minute the president called for volunteers, they came out. Those Rebels don't know what a beehive they stirred up when they turned their guns against Fort Sumter."

"The roast is cooling," Mrs. Hammer said icily.

Mr. Hammer paid no attention. Instead, he caught Annie by the elbow and said, "That's 'Yankee Doodle' they're playing, just as they did in the Revolution." Annie nodded as a fife carried the melody like a shrill voice. He pulled the drapery shut. "An old song for an old feeling, a rallying cry for a war these Rebels are forcing on us."

Without a glance at his wife, he ushered Annie to her chair. She sat stiffly as Mr. Hammer carved the roast beef.

Having eaten only a sandwich and an apple all

day, she had come to the table hungry. Still she could hardly swallow her food. How sad that this trouble that was dividing the country should also disturb the peace of this happy family.

The war was not mentioned again. The desserts were cleared away and the maid brought coffee into the drawing room. "Do forgive me, Annie, but my head is throbbing so that I must lie down," Mrs. Hammer said as she smiled wanly. "But don't let me spoil your homecoming. Sophie has some special songs to play in your honor. And rest well, my dear."

She pressed her cool cheek against Annie's and swept away, her skirts rustling mysteriously through the hall.

Sophie's fingers were deft on the harpsichord. Annie felt herself slowly relax under the rippling flow of sound. Mr. Hammer leaned toward her and spoke softly. "You must forgive Mrs. Hammer, my dear. She's under great strain. She fears that this coming conflict will rob her of her son."

Annie glanced in horror at Will. He nodded. "I am planning to join a Michigan regiment right away," he said. "I wouldn't miss this opportunity for anything."

Sophie glanced at him, lifted her hands, and brought them crashing down onto her keys. She rose, nearly throwing the bench over, and fled from the room in a storm of tears.

Annie got up, too, her heart thundering. Will

caught her hand. "Give her a little time," he said. "It probably helps her to cry. Has she talked to you about Edwin Powers?"

"She mentioned him in letters," Annie told him, sitting back down reluctantly.

"I should think so," Will said, smiling. "He's really a fine chap, Annie, and Sophie is completely gaga over him. I guess he's as mad about her. We've kept this a family secret but you're like family. Sophie and Edwin have been promised for nearly a year now."

"But surely he won't have to volunteer," Annie said.

"None of us *have to* yet," Will said quietly. "But it is our country that's at stake."

Annie found her bed in the guest room turned back with her worn gown and robe set out. The band still played outside. She stood at the window of the darkened room and watched flares dance along the streets. She thought of her father's excitement about "Honest Abe," which was what he called the man who was now president.

So much had happened since her father died. John Brown's battle against slavery had ended in his being hanged in Virginia. President Lincoln's election had raised a furious storm throughout the South. Some states were even pulling out of the Union. That wasn't the way a democracy worked. You didn't walk out on your country just because you didn't like the way a vote came out.

She hated the idea of war as much as Sophie did. But if the United States had to go to war to stay united, it would be *her* war, too, just as it would have been her father's, had he lived to see it come.

Five

April 1861

ANNIE MET EDWIN POWERS that next morning at church. Will had been right. Edwin and Sophie were *both* clearly "gaga" about each other. When Edwin was introduced to Annie, he said the right things but kept looking at Sophie. He opened his hymnbook to the right page, but sang as if the hymn were printed on Sophie's forehead. But what a good-looking couple they were! Although Sophie was tall, Edwin towered over her. He was handsome, too, with auburn hair and warm blue eyes that sparkled with fun just as Sophie's did.

Sophie had been sincere about having nothing but fun during Annie's visit. That afternoon Edwin took them for a ride through the park.

Sophie and Edwin sang and laughed together in the front seat while Will and Annie talked behind them. "Please don't feel you're stuck with me, Will," Annie told him. "I know you have friends of your own."

"You'll meet my friends, too," he told her. "But I can always see them. You and I have catching up to do."

To Annie's relief Will didn't ask much about her life back in Wisconsin. She wasn't ashamed of those years, but they were over. It had always embarrassed her when Claire told her how "heroic" she was. She had only done what had to be done, just as Belle had taught her to do.

After the ride, they had supper with Edwin's family. Later they played wonderful parlor games. Annie couldn't remember laughing so much. Edwin was a clown. Everything became a game to him. He challenged Will to an eating-and-drinking contest, which he won easily. "I yield," Will cried with a groan when Edwin started on his second gallon of cider and his third dozen of ginger cookies.

Sophie took Annie on endless shopping tours. They lunched at tearooms on tiny sandwiches and moist cakes decorated with candied violets. Annie was terrified at the prospect of a supper dance given in her honor. "I haven't danced for years! I'm not even sure I'll know how!" she wailed. Sophie just went on piling Annie's thick brown hair high under a tiny evening hat that matched the lavendar dancing dress Sophie insisted that she borrow.

Sophie stepped back to admire her handiwork. "There," she said proudly. "Just keep smiling and backing away from those men's big feet and you'll do fine."

She paused, then smiled. "Edwin will be proud to dance with such a beauty as you. He is a dream to dance with."

Edwin was no better a dancer than Will but he was easy to amuse. Annie just kept telling him how wonderful Sophie was and letting him agree with her.

"Edwin says you are terribly clever," Sophie told Annie between sets. Annie swallowed her laughter and nodded.

The whirlwind of lunches and parties and musicals and carriage rides went on all that week and over the next Sunday.

As much as Annie enjoyed being a giddy girl again, she couldn't ignore Detroit's rising pitch of war fever. At all hours the streets throbbed with bands, music, and orators.

But only Will would discuss the news with her. He claimed the situation with the South worsened daily. It was Will who told her about the first Union blood being spilled.

"It wasn't so much a battle as a riot," Will told her. "The people of Baltimore attacked a train-load of Union soldiers. Four men were killed and at least thirty-six wounded. Such business could result in the capital in Washington being cut off completely from the North."

At Annie's shocked expression, he shook his head. "Don't be like Mother, Annie. Face the facts. Nothing can stop this war now. The important thing is to win it."

"Anyway," he went on. "Within days the North will be ready to fight back. They plan to recruit a regiment here in Detroit right away. That's a thousand men, right there."

He dropped his voice. "And I'll be among them."

"Surely your family knows this," she said.

"I've tried to make it clear. Father knows. Sophie won't admit it. Mother acts as if I am saying it to upset her. Why fight with her when nothing will change my mind?"

Annie studied his face. She was suddenly aware she was envious that he had the privilege of going off to fight for what he believed in. He took her hands. "Don't look so sad. I want to do this."

She looked away. How embarrassing that he thought she had been worried about his safety when she was really only thinking of herself. "I'm not sad, Will," she admitted. "I am just so jealous that I can't stand it."

He stared at her, then laughed. "Jealous! Come now, Annie. You a soldier? You've always been terrified of guns, even locked in the case in the hall. Look at you, no taller than a cannon yourself. Besides, you *are* just a girl."

She felt her cheeks glow with angry color. "All right, Will Hammer!" Her dark eyes snapped at him. "You're right about the guns, I hate them and they scare me. And I don't claim to be any giant. But don't tell me I'm *just* a girl. My mother pioneered out here with my father. Women like her worked like men, drove oxen, pulled plows, even hunted game. You can be a female without being *just* a girl!"

"Hey, there," he soothed her. "I meant no insult. But war is different. Everyone who's involved is in danger."

"I know that. I know men get killed and wounded. Who takes care of them?"

"They have male orderlies for that," Will replied.

She shook her head. "That's a waste. They should let women do the nursing so those men could fight, too."

"Listen to you," he laughed. "How did the army ever get along without your advice?" Then he frowned at her. "If they did let you onto a battlefield, what do you know about nursing?"

She felt her color deepen. He didn't know of

her father's long, lingering illness. Nor had she told him of her care of the banker's uncle. Mentioning those hard years would only embarrass both of them. "If *you* can learn to be a soldier, *I* can learn to be a nurse. At the least, I could change beds, keep patients clean, and see that they're fed."

He shrugged. "Well, the regiment will be signing up some women, probably about twenty."

She stared at him. "What did you say?"

He shrugged. "Armies are made up of fighting men," he reminded her. "But soldiers have the needs of other men. The regiment will sign up women for what needs doing, cooking, laundressing, nursing. But not as soldiers, Annie."

At that moment Sophie called Annie from upstairs. She escaped gladly, her head spinning with this new possibility. Will had said women, but couldn't a girl work, too? If Will thought she wouldn't stoop to such menial work, he was wrong. She didn't care what she did to serve. She was as much an American as he was, wasn't she?

She had told Claire that she would recognize what she wanted when it came along. She had recognized this in a spinning moment and thought of little else from that moment on. Twenty women. Surely hundreds of women and girls would apply for those openings. And surely they would choose extraordinary people, not just ordinary girls like herself. Did she dare even dream of getting such a great opportunity?

Since that first night, Annie had been tense about another scene at Sophie's house. To her relief, the subject of war never came up when the family was together. On Wednesday, the day that Colonel Israel Richardson called for the sign-up of the 2nd Michigan Volunteer Regiment, she realized the subject was a banked fire, waiting to blaze up.

Mrs. Hammer didn't appear for breakfast. The maid served with swollen eyes. Since Will was already gone and Sophie was "indisposed," Annie had breakfast with Mr. Hammer.

"How nice for us to have some time together," Mr. Hammer said to her. "You girls have flitted about so much that I've barely seen you. I hoped we could talk about your future plans."

"You mustn't be concerned," Annie told him. "I have some work skills, and the ordinary womanly skills." She paused. Did she dare tell Sophie's father what had filled her mind these past days?

"Please, sir," she said. "May I ask something in confidence?"

He looked startled but nodded. Belle had always made a big issue of Annie staying calm and controlled. Suddenly she couldn't manage to do this. She leaned toward him, her eyes shining with excitement. "I plan to try to sign with the regiment," she told him. "Like Will, I want to serve."

"Annie!" Mr. Hammer's voice rose in shocked disbelief. "To go for a soldier? You, a mere slip of a girl?"

"Oh, no, sir. Not as a soldier," she said quickly. "They are signing up women. They call them laundresses, but Will thinks they'll do other things, too — such as nursing."

He nodded, "The French call such women Daughters of the Regiment. What an astonishing idea." He shook his head. "But my dear, what a hard life that is! Living in the field, being exposed to disease, seeing death, and perhaps even finding yourself in mortal danger."

"My circumstances would be the same as the men's. The thought of dying *does* terrify me, but the men must feel the same way," she told him. "And I'm young and strong. I want to be where I can really help people."

"A few women among those hundreds of men," he said thoughtfully. "Are you sure this is what you want?"

"I *am* sure," she told him. "The moment Will told me of this enlistment, I felt as if someone had called my name."

"Few people will understand this, Annie," he

warned. He sat in silence for a long time, then set his hand on hers. "This frightens me, Annie, but you have my blessing. If I were younger, I would enlist myself." His voice was charged with sudden emotion. He drew out a handkerchief and wiped his eyes.

Six

April 25 – 27, 1861

ANNIE WORRIED HERSELF to sleep. How could she enlist without telling Sophie what she was doing? She woke up cross at herself that next morning. What was she worrying about? Sophie was her friend, not her nursemaid. She had her own life to live and she *did* have Mr. Hammer's blessing!

She was already dressed when Sophie came to her room. "Look at you," Sophie cried. "With your hair up and all!"

"I had an errand and thought I'd do it early."

"A secret errand?" Sophie asked. "Come on, Annie, what are you up to? I saw you and Will with your heads together. You're planning to do something exciting without me."

Annie bit her lips thoughtfully. "It is exciting to me, Sophie, but it has nothing to do with Will. I didn't want to tell you until I found out whether I could do it or not."

"*Do it!*" Sophie cried. "Don't be mysterious! Do *what?*"

Annie's breath came painfully short. "Enlist with the volunteers," she said all in a rush.

Sophie grew pale and covered her mouth with both hands. "Annie," she breathed. "You can't mean that."

"Listen to me," Annie begged. "Let me explain." As Annie talked, Sophie stared at her aghast.

"You can't!" she cried. "You could be killed. We're ladies. Ladies don't do laundry, not even for the army."

Annie took Sophie's hands. "Think what you're saying, Sophie. Is my life more precious than Will's and Edwin's?"

"Edwin isn't going," Sophie said with frightful intensity. "He promised me, gave me his word of honor."

Annie hesitated. Did Sophie realize that Will had no intention of giving such a pledge? Didn't Sophie know that lots of ladylike women washed clothes and cooked for families they loved because the work needed doing?

"The enlistment is for only three months. I

really want to do this," Annie repeated over and over.

In the end, Sophie gave up. She cried and was horrified but she finally quit protesting. "But you can't go off alone," she told Annie. "We could never explain that to Mother. We'll take the buggy. She'll think it's a jaunt."

Sophie drove silently to the recruitment center. As Annie stepped down, Sophie broke down and wailed. "Mother will *never* forgive me if she discovers I helped you!"

Annie patted her hand. "And I would never forgive you if you stood in my way."

A uniformed soldier directed Annie into a cavernous room. She hesitated at the door. Milling girls crowded the space. Annie's heart sank. How could they choose only twenty from so many? The women were all sizes — slender and heavyset, tall and short. Their voices rose and fell.

A ragged line led to a desk where a sergeant was talking to the candidates. Annie got in line and watched him. He was sorting out the applicants. The women left his desk to go one way or another, out the door, or to the next desk to be interviewed again. What if she were rejected at once and sent out the door? She wondered what they had said to be turned down right away like that.

The line inched forward. Annie was handed a paper to fill out. She had just finished it when she found herself across the desk from the sergeant. Her knees trembled wildly under her long, full skirt. She knew her voice would quaver when she tried to speak.

He studied the paper a moment before looking up.

"Annie B. Etheridge," he read. "Sixteen. Full young."

"I will be seventeen in just a few days," she told him.

He studied her sternly. "I hope you don't think this is some party you are volunteering for. The work is hard and the hours long." She stiffened under his glance, trying to appear as tall and old as possible. This did little good, because he barely hid his grin. "How much use could you be, a mere handful of a girl like you?"

His words stung. How insulting for him to speak of parties when she had come to volunteer! And how tedious always to be reminded that she was no giant! The sudden flush of anger that brought color to her cheeks also made her tongue more tart than she intended.

"A wagon spring is not judged by its size," she told him, her eyes daring him to contradict her.

His eyebrows danced for a moment, then he chuckled. "I can't argue with that. And spoken in educated tones. Tell me, Annie B. Etheridge, why you have offered yourself for this service?"

"I'm a loyal citizen," she told him, meeting his eyes boldly. "That's what President Lincoln asked for."

He was silent for a moment. "A lot of women who consider themselves loyal citizens have answered me differently. Some see this as a chance to escape unhappy homes. Some are attracted by the excitement and the parades. Some admit that they hope to find husbands in the army. You simply claim to be a patriot and leave it to me to find your motive. What are *you* looking for by joining the regiment?"

Why was she letting him annoy her? It was his job to sort out weak applicants, but did he have to be sarcastic?

He stared at her, his eyes narrowed. "I repeat — the work is harsh and the hours long. An army travels light and fast. No womanly vanities or comforts. Can you endure hardships?"

"If I thought I couldn't, I wouldn't have come."

He chuckled again and shoved her paper back. "Mine isn't the final word, Annie Etheridge, but you've sold me. And such a pretty girl would be an ornament to any man's army. Your health must be checked and you have forms to fill out before we can welcome you to the Second Michigan Volunteer Regiment. Now, step to the next table, please."

Annie caught her breath and gripped his hand

hard. "Thank you, sir," she said with what breath she could muster. "Thank you. Thank you, thank you, thank you."

This time he laughed out loud. "I hope you still thank me when we reach the field of battle, Annie Etheridge."

The rest of the day spun away. She filled out questionnaires about her health, what diseases she'd had, and whether she was subject to fainting spells. The doctor who took her pulse and peered into her throat and ears grunted to himself. He signed her form and nodded her on.

She was finally released carrying a sheaf of papers. One of them was her order to report at something called Cantonment Blair with all proper dispatch.

She had enough money to hire a horse cab but she didn't hail one. She was too excited to sit still. Instead, she walked back to the Hammer house through the crowded streets, barely hearing the noise. Someone pressed a small flag into her hand. She carried it as if in a dream.

Over and again she had been thrown into circumstances that were outside of her control — her father's business failure, the move to Wisconsin, and the loss of both her father and husband. For once she was really taking control — doing what she wanted to do on her own.

Joy combined with a tingling of fear to quicken her steps. Gripping the little flag, she danced up the front stairs of the Hammer house.

Sophie was playing the harpsichord for her mother. As Mrs. Hammer glanced up at Annie, Sophie put her finger to her lips to warn her to silence.

Mrs. Hammer sounded disappointed. "Oh, it's you, Annie. Come in, dear." She rose. "I'll have some tea brewed. I can't seem to shake the chill in the air today."

The moment her mother left, Sophie flew to Annie's side. "You didn't really do it, did you?" she asked. "I knew that when you actually got there, you would realize — "

"But I did, Sophie," Annie broke in.

"You only signed up. They didn't accept you."

"But they did," Annie told her. "I am to report."

Sophie stood still a moment with her eyes closed and her hands clenched in tight fists at her side. Annie felt the effort her friend was making to control herself. She had never seen Sophie, charming, fun-loving Sophie, exert such self-control. She caught Sophie in her arms and held her tight. "Please don't grieve, Sophie," she begged. "This is something I *want* to do, something I *need* to do."

Sophie sighed and opened her eyes. Her eyelashes were wet. "I can't lose everyone I love. I can't. I just can't!" she cried in a broken voice.

When the door at the end of the hall swung open, Sophie seized Annie's hands. "Say nothing to Mother, no matter what," she whispered intensely.

"But I have to tell her *sometime*," Annie protested.

"Not now," Sophie said. "Not yet."

Before they finished their tea, the men returned. As Will and his father came to the open doorway, Mrs. Hammer stiffened in her chair. Her words came swift and almost harshly. "Very well, William, what is the news?"

Annie dropped her eyes to avoid the pain in Will's face. "I have enlisted, Mother, as I told you I must."

The silence was broken by the musical sound of Mrs. Hammer's china cup falling as she slumped to the floor.

"Quick, Will, " Mr. Hammer cried. "Help your mother up. Sophie, get smelling salts. Annie, do run like a good girl and tell the maid we need help."

Within minutes the men had assisted Mrs. Hammer to her room, half carrying her up the carpeted steps. The maid scurried behind, emitting sharp cries like a wounded animal.

Annie looked up to see Sophie staring at her across the silent hall. Bright patches of color had risen to Sophie's cheeks and her eyes blazed with anger.

"Don't you *dare* stand there and judge my mother in your heart, Annie Etheridge," she said furiously. "She's no less a patriot than you. And she's going to be doing the hard things, not you. When Will goes away she can only worry and grieve, but you'll be fine. You'll be just like a man, busy all the time, knowing what's going on. Mother and I can only wait, praying for letters, watching at windows. I only hope you suffer every bit as much as we will." Sophie turned in a whirl of petticoats and ran up the stairs after her parents.

As Annie looked after Sophie with a thundering heart, Will came down the stairs. He led her back into the drawing room. "Don't listen to her. You know how emotional she is."

Annie shook her head. "Sophie could be right, Will. The waiting might be the worst of all. And the not knowing."

Neither Sophie nor Annie mentioned the outburst again. But a brittle tension gripped the household the rest of that day and the next. There was little time for talk anyway. The house was a hubbub as Will's supplies were assembled. Annie only repacked the trunk she had brought to Detroit with her.

That Friday Mr. Hammer drove Annie and

Will out to the old Agricultural Fairground that had been turned into Cantonment Blair. When Annie looked back, Sophie stood in the doorway with her arm around her weeping mother. How cold and empty the house looked in the pale April sunlight.

Seven

May 3, 1861

ANNIE'S BIRTHDAY fell on Friday, the third of
May. She woke at dawn. The narrow barracks
room throbbed with the sleep of her companions,
deep even breathing, sometimes a sigh, Florrie's
dry cough, and the creaking of a cot. She looked
along the four rows of cots. The past few days
had been so different from anything in her life
before that they seemed more like a dream than
real life.

She had signed up in Detroit, reported to
Cantonment Blair, and already the regiment was
in the process of being transferred to Fort Wayne,
near Detroit. She was still only learning the names
of the girls she shared the room with.

The blonde girl named Ellie was too loud and

51

outspoken to go unnoticed. Betsy, the tall one with the red hair, was more tactful but just as aggressive. How different the girls all were — Sarah, with the quiet smile; Carrie, whose low laughter made Annie feel cheerful; and Florrie, who hadn't said two words that Annie had heard.

Never mind. She would have time to make friends later. For now, she wasn't close enough to any of them to mention how special this day was to her.

The wake-up call launched the race against the morning schedule. Wash. Dress. Spruce up the barracks. Swallow breakfast and spill out into the morning chill. As they gathered for the morning briefing, Annie saw Will Hammer approaching. How wonderful to see him. How tall and tan he looked, striding toward her. He leaned to kiss her cheek and handed her a small package tied with a red ribbon. "With love from us all," he said. "Happy birthday, Annie. And a book from Father with his blessing."

She held the gifts, close to tears from delight. "Oh, Will," she said. "It's present enough just to see you." With more than a thousand men crowded in the camp, she felt lucky even to glimpse him from a distance. She barely had time to thank him before he strode off briskly.

The girls clustered around her. "Is that your man then?" Carrie asked, staring after Will. "Handsome I say!"

"Open up, let's see the present," Sarah said.

"We should have guessed this quiet one was hiding secrets from us," Ellie said.

Annie felt herself flush. Why did Ellie have to call her "this quiet one" in that sneering way? Just because she didn't chatter all the time didn't mean that she was unfriendly. She had learned from their conversations that many of them were used to being around a group of people. Polly was full of stories about the customers at the inn her family ran on the post road north. Liz, the most efficient worker Annie had ever seen, talked wistfully about her seven younger brothers and sisters.

Not only was Annie an only child, but she had spent a lot of time alone in the past few years. Sometimes she was completely overwhelmed with the exuberance of the crowd of girls. They were full of talk of men and clothes and the excitement of travel. But some of the things they said bothered her. When she really listened to their talk, she wondered if they had enlisted to serve their community or just get away from home for a grand adventure.

"Hurry up," Ellie said. "We haven't got all day."

Annie untied the ribbon with trembling fingers, embarrassed at this attention. Seeing Will again had made her lonely for her old friends. "This is from his family," she said. "We're very good friends, and today is my birthday."

"Well, happy birthday, indeed," Ellie said, taking the tiny sewing kit from her hand. The dainty present was passed from hand to hand while the girls fussed over its contents. Annie was sure Sophie had made the kit herself. The green velvet case was designed to fold flat and be tied with a sturdy ribbon. It held everything she could need — small scissors with embossed handles, needles and thread, even a row of camisole buttons.

"It's beautiful," Carrie said. "How nice to have such thoughtful friends."

"And how many years do you claim?" Betsy asked.

"Seventeen," Annie told her.

Betsy threw her head back and laughed. Loudly. "Listen to that. For myself I will claim seventeen only when I am safe with hearth and husband."

Annie smiled and tucked the sewing kit into her skirt pocket, nodding at the chorus of birthday wishes. Betsy was twenty if she was a day, but that was no concern of hers. It was enough that *she* was seventeen this very day and going to war for her country!

Since no one had shown any interest in the book Mr. Hammer had sent, she waited until she was alone to unwrap it. She almost cried out with pleasure to see *Notes on Nursing*, by Florence

Nightingale. This was a famous book, much sought after by many wives and mothers. She opened the note from Sophie's father.

"To our Annie," he had written in his wonderful spidery hand. *"Always a lover of new knowledge."* She held the book tightly, overwhelmed by his thoughtfulness.

The camp was a busy noisy place the entire month. All day the firing range rattled with the sound of bullets. Drill sergeants shouted orders and roared with fury at the untidy lines of farm boys they were trying to make into soldiers. Since they had no bayonets, they drilled with sharp sticks tied to their guns. As if all that noise wasn't enough to drive the birds from the trees, the regimental band practiced or marched from sunup to sundown.

The girls worked long days just as the soldiers did.

Fresh laundry appeared daily in the wash tent. Sheets, towels, trousers, stockings, and shirts grew into mountains if the girls slowed even a little. Annie had secretly hoped to make at least one close friend among these girls. But there wasn't much time to talk bending over a washboard into a tub of steaming water. By evening she was too tired to do anything but collapse onto her cot to sleep.

After the first day, Liz traded tubs with the

girl next to Annie. When Annie glanced over, Liz grinned at her.

"I've been watching you," Liz said. "If I can work with someone else who knows what she's doing, maybe I won't bite any heads off."

Annie laughed. "You don't look violent."

"I'm usually not," Liz admitted. "But I've helped raise too many little brothers and sisters to watch someone do a job halfway without setting her straight."

Annie and Liz made a good team. When they loaded a basket of wash, they carried it out to the lines together.

"This is the part I really like," Annie told Liz as a fresh breeze whipped a line of sweet-smelling clothes.

Liz nodded. "I miss my little brother Charlie though," she said with a note of hunger in her voice. "He's only four but he's always burning to be helpful. He loved running along beside me with a grape basket full of pins, chattering like a blue jay every step of the way."

When the laundry dried, the garments needing mending were set aside. Annie and the others darned stockings and sewed torn seams until the call rang for the evening meal.

"I don't know why I even go to supper," Ellie groaned, getting to her feet. "I haven't had a bite worth eating since I got to this place."

"You could volunteer to help cook," Liz suggested.

Ellie laughed. "You have to be joking. I have to be dragged into a kitchen."

Liz looked after her thoughtfully. "She doesn't like doing washing. She has to be dragged into a kitchen. What do you suppose she's good at?"

Annie grinned to herself. The answer was "complaining" but she wasn't going to say it. "Maybe nursing," she suggested.

"I think we need some of that around here right now," Liz said quietly.

Annie looked up at her.

"Have you noticed that quiet little Florrie?" Liz asked. "She's as thin as a rail and coughs all night every night. This work is too heavy for her."

Annie said nothing. Florrie's cough had haunted her from the first. Sometimes she had even wakened in the night, thinking she was back home in Wisconsin with her father coughing that same way in his dark, little room.

Ellie wasn't the only complainer. Many of the girls did only what work was absolutely necessary and this to a chorus of complaints. They criticized every bite of food put before them even though the men of the regiment sometimes only had hardtack and dried beef to sustain them. They never got enough sleep. Their backs ached. Their hands would never be soft and white again after all this washing! Others were homesick, reading letters from home with streaming eyes.

The regiment was officially mustered in on May twenty-fifth. That same day, Florrie collapsed on the way to the mess tent. Annie ran to her side and lifted her head. Liz strode through the cluster of girls crowded around them.

"Stand back," she ordered. "Give the poor girl air."

Florrie roused and began to cough, her thin body racked by the effort. Annie braced her to a sitting position as Liz held a handkerchief to her lips. "Get us some help," Liz ordered Carrie who was leaning over them.

The sturdy young orderly barely glanced at Florrie before lifting her into his arms. As he set off toward the barracks, Liz silently showed Annie the blood-stained handkerchief she had held to Florrie's lip. Annie covered her face, trying to forget her father's slow, painful death.

Eight
Washington, D.C.
1861

BEFORE THE REGIMENT left for Washington on the sixth of June, Florrie was sent back home. Ellie was furious when she learned the details of Florrie's illness. "What kind of nerve is that?" she asked angrily. "She had to know she had consumption when she signed up. Was she trying to kill us?"

"I slept next to her," Betsy wailed. "I could get it."

"Oh, both of you shut up!" Liz said fiercely. "Do you think that little girl *wanted* to get sick and probably die?"

Annie had spent a lot of time with Florrie after she fell ill. While Annie was packing Florrie's trunk, the girl had explained to Annie why she had signed up.

"I've never done anything for anyone else since I was born," Florrie told her. "Before I left this earth I wanted to do *something* worthwhile." Her dark eyes were haunted with grief. "Do you know what I mean, Annie?"

Annie nodded. She knew, but what could she say? How unfair that Florrie's time had been so brief and painful.

During their stay at Fort Wayne, Annie had made more friends than she had ever had in her life. While a lot of these were homesick soldiers, there were other women, too. She especially noticed Jane Hinsdale, whose husband Hiram was a private in Company D. Jane was a lively happy girl who threw herself into enjoying camp life just as her husband did.

Annie sometimes ran into the sergeant who signed her up. He always grinned and asked the same question, "Are you still telling me thank you, Annie Etheridge?"

Although she had seen little of his wife, Colonel Israel Richardson was too colorful to miss. He was a tall man with a mustache as drooping as his carriage was erect. If he had chosen to stride around camp with the arrogance of some of the lesser officers, he would have put them all to shame. Instead he wore a battered straw hat and strolled around with his hands in his pockets, looking for all in the world like a farmer out to enjoy the scenery.

Since his rank was seldom visible, he was often mistaken for an orderly by a green young officer. Annie loved the way he laughed and didn't take offense at being bossed about by an underling.

Annie kept hoping that she and the other girls would get some nursing training. Lacking this, she studied the Florence Nightingale book Sophie's father had given her.

Polly picked the book up one evening, only to throw it back down in disgust. "From the way you were eating this up I figured it was some exciting romance. Why do you want to read about sick people and bloody wounds?"

"We'll be where men get hurt," Annie reminded her. "I want to learn as much about nursing as I can."

"I didn't sign up to do nursing," Ellie said. "I can't stand sick people, and the smell of blood makes me vomit."

Annie only looked at her, but Liz's question came back to her mind. Indeed, what *did* Ellie like to do?

By the time the regiment left for Washington, D.C., the 2nd Michigan Volunteers were signed up for three years. Annie didn't care. She felt as much a part of the regiment as any man who drilled and practiced on the firing range.

With a thousand men in the regiment Annie

seldom saw Will Hammer, but he looked her up when their regiment was assigned to the Army of the Potomac. "But that's the river that runs by Washington," Annie said.

"Exactly," Will said. "The enemy territory starts on the other side of that river. Our army is assigned to defend the capital city. It's the most important assignment."

Annie had looked forward to seeing the capital. She hadn't expected the confusion she found. Washington was crammed. Long, dusty lines of military wagons snaked through the streets alongside troops wearing uniforms of every description. In among them wove hurrying couriers and officers on horses that were skittish from the hubbub. It was a great relief to escape with her regiment to Camp Winfield Scott in Washington Heights.

They had been in Washington only a week when Liz came to Annie with tears in her eyes. She sat a moment, fighting to control herself before trying to speak. Annie took her hand and waited.

Finally, Liz shook her head and whispered, "I can't even tell you. Here, read for yourself."

The letter began, "My dearest Elizabeth." Annie read the neatly written lines with growing horror. Liz's mother had delivered a stillborn child and failed to recover her strength. "I can't tell you how deeply sorry I am to call you home, dear daughter," the letter went on. "But as you know, no one but you can hold our family together."

"Oh, Liz," Annie cried, dropping the letter to take her friend in her arms. "I am so sorry, so very sorry."

Liz nodded, the tears streaming down her face, "It's not that I don't want to help at home," she wept. She hugged Annie tight. "Oh, I will miss you so, Annie. You will have to do for the two of us what we would have done together."

"I will," Annie whispered. "You know I will try."

It wasn't the same with Liz gone. It was hot. The city smelled, even from camp, like an open sewer. The flies were so thick that you had to scrape them off your food. Had they hurried here to wait forever? Why should they endlessly wash clothes for men who did nothing but march back and forth and sweat them dirty again?

One June night as the girls were preparing for bed, Betsy leapt from her cot, strode across the room, and slammed the window shut. "What's the matter with you?" Ellie called, rising on one elbow. "We'll suffocate in this place without that breeze."

"I just want to shut out that stupid singing," Betsy told her. "It's about to drive me crazy."

Ellie got up and opened the window again. She stood listening to the distant voices of the singing soldiers. "Even that's better than dying of the heat."

"It's going to be a lot hotter than this when we go marching down into the South," Carrie said.

"Marching?" Betsy cried, sitting up to stare at her. "We won't march. We'll ride along in wagons."

Carrie giggled softly. "It's not funny," Betsy said angrily. "It's as if everybody were trying to talk me out of this army. I didn't leave three meals a day to tramp around like a horse, any more than I did to nurse people."

The Fourth of July brought parades and speeches and marching to the regimental band. Even in the noonday heat Annie loved marching behind their regimental flag. The magnificent silk flag had been handmade by the women of Niles, Michigan. Annie watched its gleaming folds ripple in the sun and thought about the love and patriotism stitched into those stars and bars.

Sarah, watching Annie, spoke softly to keep anyone from hearing her question. "Are you really going through with this?" she asked in a hesitant voice.

Annie stared at her. "Going through with what?"

"Staying with the army," Sarah sounded exasperated. "This is nothing like I expected and the worst hasn't come yet. One of the men said we were going into battle in Virginia right away, bullets and cannons and everything."

"That's what we all signed up for," Annie reminded her.

Sarah shook her head. "*You* might have. We've talked it over and the minute this regiment is called to the field, this little lady is taking herself back home to Detroit."

At Annie's shocked expression, Sarah snorted. "I'm not the only one. I bet we'll *all* pack back to Michigan. And that can't happen soon enough for me."

"But what of the men?" Annie asked, unable to believe what she was hearing.

"Let them find girls of their own to slave for them," she said. "You've seen Colonel Richardson's wife in her fancy clothes and ruffled bonnet. You don't see *her* or the other wives putting their hands to a washboard, do you?"

When Annie didn't reply, Sarah repeated the question angrily. "Do you? Now, do you?"

As much as Annie hated arguments, she had to answer the insistent question. "It's not the same thing," she said. "The wives have simply come to be with their husbands. We *signed up* to work for this regiment."

The girl stared at her with narrowed eyes. "If you're serious then you're crazy. How will it look when you go off to war with over a thousand men?"

Annie felt her cheeks flush with anger. The girl had asked for an answer and she was just going to get it. "How's it going to look for eighteen Michigan girls to live on the army, travel on the army, and then run home with their tails between their legs at the first sign of danger?"

That evening in the barracks, Sarah goaded Annie again to go along with the others in leaving. Not wanting to argue, she said nothing. When the other girls chimed in, Annie had enough. She grasped her skirt and fled from the room for fear she would say more than she meant to.

"Snit," Sarah shouted after her. "Dowdy little self-satisfied snit!"

Outside, Annie caught her breath and slowed to a walk. She knew Sarah called her dowdy because of her skirts. The minute they reached camp she had packed her wire hoop crinoline away because it got in her way at work. If she ever needed it, she only had to dig it from her trunk.

The enlisted men were cooking their evening meals. The scent of wood smoke perfumed the air. A soldier strummed a guitar and sang about the girl he had left behind him.

The voice at her elbow startled her. "Are you all right, Annie Etheridge?" the soldier asked.

She looked up at him. "How did you know my name?"

He laughed. "There's a lot of us men and not

66

very many of you girls," he reminded her. "We know your name especially because you're the prettiest."

"Thank you," Annie said, flustered by the compliment.

"Is something wrong? You came flying out of there like you were trying to outrun bees."

Annie laughed. "If it had been bees, I would still be running," she said. "I'm fine, thank you."

He fell into step. "How do you like Washington?"

Annie wished he hadn't asked. She had listened to the girls complain so much that she wouldn't do that.

"It will be pretty when they finish that Capitol dome. And I've never ever seen so many people together." She paused. "Forgive me but I don't know your name."

He lifted his cap. "Private Flint Franklin Thompson, field nurse, Company F. I hear good things about you."

"Thank you, Private Thompson," she said.

"Just call me Frank," he said. "Most folks do."

She nodded. "And my friends call me Annie." He was short for a man, with large, dark eyes. His cheeks were as smooth as if he were still beardless. He smiled as he walked along beside her in an easy comfortable gait.

Frank was better company than the girls, now that Liz was gone. Besides, he was full of news

67

about the war and how the campaigns were going.
At dusk, he walked her home.

"You're mighty easy to talk to," he said. Then
he winked. "But remember I've told you no tales
out of school."

Nine

Blackburn's Ford
July 16 – 18, 1861

WHEN ANNIE WAS LITTLE, "telling tales out of school" had meant giving away secrets. What had Frank said during their walk that could possibly have any secret meaning? Nothing had changed! The bugs still hung in clouds, the water was too foul to drink, and Annie could only breathe the air when she dabbed herself with cologne.

Then suddenly the number of reporters and photographers in the camp doubled. The drills all went to fast time, and the bands played so briskly that the drummers made their sticks dance in the air. Just as Annie thought she was going to *explode* with curiosity, the mystery was solved. The marching orders came!

Had Frank somehow learned General Tyler's plans in advance? The Union Army, thirty-four thousand men strong, was to march on July sixteenth. Annie was filled with excitement. The waiting was over. At last they could do what they had come so far to do!

When Annie reached the barracks the girls were in an uproar. Ellie was shouting, and Betsy was almost as loud. Even the quieter girls were adding their voices. Shirts and skirts and capes and petticoats were everywhere, folded on cots, draped over the backs of chairs, and piled into open trunks.

Annie smiled. Now she knew the girls had just been teasing her. They had planned to serve with the regiment all the time, just as she had. She crossed to her own cot, wondering if they had the same quivery feelings of fear that she had.

Ellie, leaning over her trunk, glanced up. "Look at her!" she said. "What are you here for, Etheridge?"

Annie stared. "I heard the orders and came to pack."

"To go marching off, I guess," Betsy said scathingly. Annie looked at her and then around the room. They were *all* glaring at her. What had she done? Then it struck her. It wasn't anything she had *done*. It was what she was *doing*.

70

"Anything to make the rest of us look bad," Ellie said.

Annie worked silently, folding her clothes. Only with her bonnet on and her trunk packed, did she answer them.

"Nobody has to make you look bad," she told them. "You are managing to do that all by yourselves." With that, she marched out of the door.

Later, when Annie's trunk was loaded onto the regiment wagon, she saw the girls' things being set on a horse-drawn cart. Betsy was the last to get her trunk up. She turned, tugging her glove, and shook her head at Annie.

"You know you are crazy, don't you?" she asked.

How could she answer a question like that? Annie turned away, not even wishing them a safe journey home. In fact, it wouldn't hurt her feelings a bit if they had a *miserable* trip back home! A sharp corkscrew of fear twisted in her stomach. So she was a little afraid. But surely no more than the men of the regiment were.

The army in motion was a river of men. The columns flowed out of the city too fast for the covered wagon trains of supplies and ammunition to be organized.

Annie and Sophie had *always* loved parades.

71

What would Sophie say to this one marching forth into Virginia? New to the military, Annie hadn't realized that her regiment would be combined with others to form a brigade, and these joined for a division. Since the volunteers had been mustered too fast to have uniforms made, each regiment provided its own. One New York regiment marched in bright plaid trousers. The all-Irish 69th New York Zouaves wore red Turkish trousers and fezzes and marched under an emerald green flag. The feathers on the hats of the Garibaldi Guard glistened.

Annie laughed. Maybe she was crazy to be tramping along the road with this wild colorful army, but it was wonderful in spite of the blazing sun. Almost at once, sweat trickled down Annie's back. Within a mile, every stitch she wore clung wetly to her skin. But at least she wasn't carrying a heavy musket like the men were.

A few miles out of Alexandria an orderly trotted up leading a sweating horse. "There you are," he said. "You're so little I almost missed you." He dropped to her side and offered his hand for her to mount the extra horse.

"I don't understand," she said. "Whose horse is that?"

"I was told to lend it to Annie Etheridge, the Daughter of the Regiment."

"Oh," Annie cried. "I can march if the men can."

He shook his head. "Colonel Richardson's orders. You have to ride. Why, if you lost your footing, the entire regiment could march right over you without realizing it."

"I'm not *that* short," she protested, smiling.

"Anyway, we can't spare you. Quick, now, up you go."

Annie obeyed, draping her sidesaddle skirt carefully over the horse's sweating flank. "Now," the orderly said, handing her two pistols. "These are for your belt."

"Oh, no. I hate guns," she said, shivering.

"That's an order, too," he said. "You'll only need them if you fall into Rebel hands. And neither of us want that, do we?" He watched her thrust the guns in under her belt.

"Now the last thing." He laid two bulging saddlebags across her mount's back. "We call these the pillboxes. They're filled with lint and bandages — things you'll need if we have wounded," he explained. Then he winked. "Probably Johnny Reb will turn tail and run at the sight of us. But if he doesn't, you'll wish you had them."

He cantered off, waving before he disappeared. Riding *was* easier than walking in that intense heat. Annie's horse lifted her above most of the dust raised by the marching army. Her throat was dry with thirst but she wasn't alone in this. The men ignored the shouts of their officers and broke ranks to search for water along the road.

Lulled by the horse's easy gait, Annie thought about the girls she had enlisted with. Betsy had called her crazy. Even Sophie had called her enlistment a crazy idea. Why was she so certain she was doing the right thing? Thirsty as they were, the men began to sing. First a dozen voices, then a hundred joined in. Annie hummed along.

The first day's march took them to the Fairfax County Courthouse. The men were still making evening coffee when Annie rolled herself in her blanket and went dead asleep. On the second day these untried civilians carried their muskets with aching arms. Their destination, the town of Centerville, was deserted. The town boasted only a boxlike stone church and a few rundown houses. Everything was locked up tight and the Confederate trenches around the town were empty.

As Annie watched the men search the deserted town, Fred Wustenberg from her regiment joined her. "That horse must be plenty tired of you," he said, offering her a hand to dismount.

"No tireder than I am of him," Annie replied, springing down beside him. "And both of us could use a little water."

As the horse drank hungrily, she looked at Fred. "What comes next?"

"The general needs to find out how many

Confederate troops are down at Bull Run. It's only a few miles farther."

Annie nodded. "Have they sent out scouts?"

He shook his head. "He's sending out a reconnaissance in force — an entire brigade — ours."

Something leaped in Annie's chest. Was it excitement or fear? It didn't matter. This was what she had come to do.

"You probably need to stay at the rear." Fred said.

She shook her head. "I am going along with you."

He looked at her intently, then shrugged. "That's an argument I don't want to take on."

They rode out about noon, accompanied by a squadron of cavalry and a single battery of artillerymen. An orderly reined in beside Annie and offered her his canteen. The water was warm, but Annie drank it gratefully. "Where are we going?" Annie asked him.

"There are fords and bridges all along this Bull Run Creek," he said. "We're headed for the one they call Blackburn's Ford. We're just feeling out the Rebs."

When he cantered off ahead, Annie followed, suddenly cold with fear. She distracted herself from her own terrified thoughts by studying the land around her.

Beyond the level bottomland on the run at Blackburn's Ford stretched the forest. Not since Wisconsin had she seen such dense stands of trees. Even under the brilliant noonday sun, the shade was deep enough to conceal an entire army.

As Annie's horse rested first one foot and then the other, Annie stared into that ominous leafy darkness. She watched a cannon being hauled up onto an open elevation.

"How can they tell what to fire at?" she asked the soldier at her side. "All I can see is leafy green."

"They can't," he told her. "They'll just fire it off and hope to locate the enemy's position."

The gunners set the twenty-pound cannon and loaded it. At a brisk order, Lieutenant Edwards fired at random into the dark woods. Annie stifled a cry as her horse reared in sudden panic at the vibration of the cannon. As she fought to control her mount, the air turned rank with the stench of gunpowder.

An enemy battery instantly returned the fire. Two cavalry horses were struck by the grapeshot. They screamed in agony, threw off their riders, and thrashed wildly on the ground before lying still. Two men had also fallen to the shot. Annie wheeled her horse and plunged into the confusion to reach their sides. Why had she ever thought she was prepared? The sight of the first

76

soldier writing on the ground, clutching his chest with his one good arm, brought sudden, hot tears to her eyes. His other arm dangled limply, staining his uniform scarlet with blood.

"I'm shot," he cried out as if surprised. "I'm shot, that's what I am, shot."

If she couldn't *feel* brave, she at least had to act it. "Try to hold firm," Annie told him. Her fingers trembled as she loosened his collar and unfastened his shirt to expose his chest. After packing lint into his small wounds, she bandaged his torn shoulder.

"Can you stand up?" she asked him, taking his good arm.

He looked at her, his eyes dark with anger. "You bet I can stand up. What's more I can fight. No sneaking Johnny Reb is going to knock me out of this war on the first day."

Once on his feet, he wavered, but staggered stubbornly toward the rear of the skirmish line. Annie breathed a deep sigh of relief as she moved on to the next victim. As Annie rose from bandaging the second soldier, she heard the bugler signal a charge as the regimental flag was unfurled.

Anne felt her courage drain away again. A charge. It was one thing for them to be struck by a few shells. To charge meant to hurl themselves into the enemy in force. Annie held her breath as she mounted to ride. The brigade plunged forward with such force that two of the mounted officers rode through the Confederate line. Both men instantly fell to enemy guns. The Confederate fire was swift and deadly. Eighty men fell during the three-hour battle that followed.

There was no time to think or feel. Annie worked like a machine, her hands swift and her mind shut tight against the pain and horror. Later when she learned that one of the militia regiments had retreated to Centreville in panic, she understood the terror that had made them run. In the midst of the fray, a mounted officer caught Annie's reins. "Go back!" he shouted. "Take cover to the rear."

She stared at him. Go back for what? She jerked her horse away and plunged recklessly forward among the advancing soldiers. What kind of an example would she give as Daughter of the Regiment if she didn't have the courage of the best of them?

And there was work to do. With the bullets and shells whining around her, she labored over the wounded. She could hardly breathe. The sickly smell of blood mingling with the odor of gunpowder made her stomach heave.

Time stood still. She felt as if she had always been in the midst of this horror and would be there forever. Deafened by gunfire and the shouts of the men, she saw her hands working without her even willing them to. As she held water to the lips of a dying soldier, the Union forces were ordered to withdraw.

Withdraw? A withdrawal was only another word for retreat. With a heavy heart, she obeyed the orders along with the others.

Ten

First Battle of Bull Run
July 21, 1861

AFTER THE RETREAT the army camped around
Centreville. The wounded men lay moaning in
the bleak stone church. Annie and the male
orderlies worked among them until the patients
fell silent except for an occasional outcry from a
painful dream.

Well after midnight Annie stepped from the
church into the open air. The heat was still
intense. Smoke from the evening campfires hung
in air too still even to stir the leaves of the trees.
Aside from fire embers, the only light came from
the flickering candles in the tents of officers still
pouring over their maps. She glared toward the
tents of the reporters. As much as she enjoyed
reading newspapers, the reporters following the

army made her angry. They were all able-bodied men! Why didn't they shoulder arms and fight like other patriots? Some of them had even pestered her while she worked with her wounded patients.

"Don't write about *me*," she had told them. "The men make your news."

Insects hummed in the darkness and a night bird called. Now and then a horse stamped or neighed softly. Annie turned with surprise when someone called her name. Frank Thompson stepped out of the darkness, his face lined with exhaustion.

"I saw you out there leading the fray," he said. "It's not going to help anybody to have you shot down."

"What could I do to help back in the rear?" she asked.

"I thought you girls were brought in to do laundry," he teased. "Does that mean washing out wounds and cleaning up battlefields?"

Annie grinned at him. "A job is what you make of it."

He looked at her thoughtfully. "Have you eaten?"

"Salt pork and hardtack earlier," she said. "I'm fine."

"I've been foraging," he said. He pulled some green apples from his pocket. "Care to risk a bellyache?"

Annie bit into the hard fruit and sucked the sour juice gratefully. "I won't really eat it, but it's wonderful," she told him.

"Do you know how many casualties there are?" he asked quietly.

She nodded, unable to meet his eyes. "Two dead, as you probably know," she said. "And we have eighty wounded."

"And at least one missing," he said quietly.

She looked the question at him.

"Mrs. Hinsdale," he told her. "She came looking for her husband and was captured by the Rebs."

Annie caught a sharp breath, thinking of the pistols she had worn into battle against just such an event. "What will happen to her?" she asked.

"What will happen to any of us?" Frank countered. Annie looked up at the sound of a sharp cry coming from inside the church. She thanked Frank again for the apple and gathered her skirts to run back to her patients.

Through the next day and night most of McDowell's Union Army camped around Centreville. The heat was so intense that the men stripped the woods to build brush shelters to shield themselves from the blazing sun.

"Tomorrow," Frank told her. "We'll have a bang-up battle tomorrow. Just you wait and see."

Waiting was all that anyone could do.

That night the regiments began to sing, their

voices rising and falling with the whimsy of the wind. The strains of "Tenting Tonight" drifted over the hills, haunting the deepening twilight. The moon hung cold and silent and a whip-poorwill sang from the dark of the woods.

When the slow notes of the bugles signaled night, the sea of men ebbed to a restless silence. In the morning General McDowell would lead his Union Army against the Confederate Army led by General Beauregard. The two men had been classmates at West Point.

The army moved out before dawn. Annie's regiment, having suffered such losses at Blackburn's Ford, was held in reserve. From the doorway of the stone church Annie watched the troops go by. Annie smiled with delight when the 1st Rhode Island Regiment passed. Kady Brownell, the daughter of *that* regiment, carried the colors. Kady dressed like no one else in the army. The daughter of a Scottish military man, Kady wore trousers with a short, bright kiltlike skirt over the top. For a belt she wore a long scarf whose tassels flipped as she marched. What Kady Brownell lacked in beauty, she made up in spirit. Small and stocky, with her dark hair loose to the wind, she marched along briskly, bearing the heavy flag standard as strongly as any man.

By ten that morning Annie heard the first thunder of battle. The wounded groaned in their beds at the sound. As she knelt by a soldier's pallet, he looked up at her. "This is a first time, Annie," he told her. "The first time two American armies have faced each other in battle."

"What about the fall of Fort Sumter?" Anne asked, removing his saturated dressing. He winced with pain.

"No blood was spilled," he reminded her, watching her deft hands clean the fresh red blood from his own wound.

Annie's regiment was called in late that day to cover the retreat of the Union Army. It was not so much a retreat as a panic. The volunteer soldiers, unprepared for this bath of death and horror, simply threw down their weapons and ran. Numb with despair, Annie ignored the screams and confusion around her and knelt beside a fallen Union soldier. She barely glanced at the unconscious figure in Confederate gray who lay only a few feet away.

"Annie," the Union soldier whispered.

"Well, hello," she said, recognizing him from back at Fort Wayne. She tried to fit a tourniquet on his mangled left arm and smile at him at the same time. "Fred Wustenberg, isn't it?"

He made a face at the pressure of the bandage and nodded. She finally stopped the flow of blood and helped him to his feet by bracing his weight against herself. "Now," she said. "I have a little present for you. You're going to ride this horse to a doctor. Let me help you up."

He was horrified. "I'm not leaving you here on foot."

"Listen to me, Fred. That arm needs a surgeon. Put your foot in my hand and mount. He's not my horse anyway. I was just lucky enough to catch him as he ran by me."

With Annie bracing him and promising him that she would be safe, he finally obeyed. Annie slapped the horse's flank. Fred slumped in the saddle, clinging with his one good hand.

As the soldiers streamed around her, white-faced and wide-eyed, she looked back at the soldier in gray. She knew she couldn't possibly know a Confederate soldier but she felt as if she did. He looked like a dozen Wisconsin farm boys she had known. A shock of pale straw-colored hair stuck straight up where his cap had fallen back. His blue eyes stared sightlessly at the sky, and his expression tugged at her heart. He looked puzzled, as if he had been asked a question he didn't know how to answer.

She dropped to her knees beside him. She lifted his wrist but could find no pulse. The coolness of his hand flooded her with sudden tears.

All she had heard about Southerners was bad. The men had a dozen insulting names for them — "Reb" being the kindest. But this was no monster. This was a simple boy that somebody loved, like Will Hammer, or Fred Wustenberg, or Frank Thompson. He had to believe in what he was fighting for, the same as she did, or he wouldn't be lying dead under a blazing sun on a bloody Virginia battlefield.

Blinking the tears from her eyes, she closed his gently. Then she touched his cheek with the palm of her hand the way his own mother might have done if she had found him here. As Mrs. Hammer would have touched Will in farewell.

As she rose, a cavalryman swung toward her, shouting, "Annie, you fool!" Leaning from his saddle, he caught her under her arms and pulled her up behind him on the saddle. "Retreat means *Go!*" Annie rode behind the cavalryman in a nightmare that lasted until dawn. Soldiers, crazed with terror, fought each other for a place in a wagon or cart, or ran mindlessly along the crowded road. The hired ambulance drivers fled with empty wagons, leaving the wounded and dying on the ground behind them. A running man fell under the wheels of one of the caissons, screaming as he was crushed to death.

Annie leaned against the cavalryman's broad back, too grieved even to cry, too heartbroken to sleep. Some time in the night it began to rain, a slow, sullen rain. It drenched the demoralized army that fed like a sluggish river down Pennsylvania Avenue into Washington.

Annie was tired. She was wet to the skin and her clothes felt as if they were weighted with

bricks from the moisture. What she *really* wanted
was a hot bath, fresh clothes, and to bury her
head in a pillow forever. And mashed potatoes.
What she wouldn't give for a serving of hot,
buttery mashed potatoes heaped on a china plate
and buried under rich golden chicken gravy!

The rain kept falling all that next day. The
city of Washington was in turmoil. Nothing was
organized. The soldiers lay in the open, muddy
streets, having no other place to go. Now and
then Annie saw men from her own regiment.

Annie, looking at this awful mess, thought of
Belle, back home. She could almost hear Belle's
voice, raspy but tender, echoing in her mind.
"When you see what's to do, do it!"

Some nurses had come from the nearby hospital to work among the men. Annie watched
them only a few minutes before straightening
her back.

"All right, Belle," she whispered crossly to the
voice she kept hearing inside her head. "I'm
going! I'm going! But that doesn't mean I *want*
to."

Eleven
July 1861

LONG TABLES had been set up inside the hospital. Behind them frantic volunteer women handed out medical supplies. Annie walked up to a dark-eyed woman. "You look ready to drop, child," she told Annie. "Must you go back out there?"

When Annie nodded and smiled, the woman filled her pillbox with fresh supplies. Annie forgot her fatigue once she was busy again. As she knelt by the soldiers, men and women leaned over to look hungrily into the wounded men's faces, searching for their missing loved ones. The pain in their faces as they turned away made Annie's heart ache.

She had always thought of the city of Washington as "Southern in sympathy." The city might be, but its women were warm and wonderful. Many came out of their houses and into the streets. Some came with servants carrying coffee and food to the wounded strangers crowding their curbstones. They brought white fabric that looked as if they had torn their own household linen into strips to make bandages.

A girl who couldn't have been twenty knelt by Annie. How soiled and unkempt Annie felt by contrast. The girl smelled of lavender and her bright hair fell in springlike curls under her bonnet. Annie almost cried to see the girl's blue silk skirt soaking up the mud of the street.

"I want to help," the girl said swiftly. "I really want to help but I don't even know how to make bandages." Her tone was as fearful as it was pleading.

"I'll show you," Annie said, taking the linen from her hand. The wounded boy stared silently from one of them to the other as Annie dressed the boy's bleeding arm.

Sweat stood on the boy's forehead from the pain, but he smiled anyway. "I know it'll heal if you stay there where I can see you," he told the girl in blue.

Annie laughed softly at the girl's sudden blush. Later that afternoon she saw the girl again, this time leading a man with a bandaged head up the wide stairs and into the front door of what must have been her own family's home.

Annie didn't see Kady Brownell striding toward her until she spoke. Kady's blouse was wet and her tasseled belt drooped to the hem of her trousers. "I've come to get you," she told Annie. "You're to come along with me."

Annie glanced at her in confusion. "What do you want?"

"You," Kady said. "And this is important! I mean, really important." Kady led Annie up a broad stairway and into a beautiful brick house. Annie looked around for someone who needed her. Instead she found herself in a room with deep wicker chairs and a table set with a silver service. The sandwich tray beside it was covered by a glass dome. The air was heavy with the scent of strong coffee.

"There," Kady said with a note of triumph. "I have kidnapped you on orders of the woman of this house. She is confined to a chair," Kady explained. "She's watched you from her window all day. She sent her servant to ask me to bring you here to rest."

"But there's so much more to do," Annie said.

Kady shook her head and gave Annie a little shove, sending her back into a tufted wicker chair. "No arguments," she said firmly. "You are to eat and drink and dry off. Do you really need a case of pneumonia?"

Annie wriggled in the soft chair, unbelievably comfortable against the soft cushions. "Not really," she admitted, not even tempted to move anymore.

The coffee was as good as it smelled. When Annie had finished two thick cheese sandwiches, Kady set her plate aside. "That dress would take too long to fix but at least you can dry your hair."

Kady sounded so much like Belle that Annie giggled. She took the pins from her hair, shook it loose, and began to rub it with the thick towel Kady handed her.

Kady grinned over at her. "You look better already," she said. "We were a pair of drowned cats."

As Kady dried her own hair, she told Annie about being caught in the thick of the battle. "I went into the field with a bunch of sharpshooters," she said. "The men advanced toward the enemy into the pinewoods. I had to stay in the open where they could see the flag." She shook her head. "Annie, you couldn't have heard thunder! Shells whined over my head and the enemy guns were hammering back at our artillery. And all the time their regiments were moving up.

"A little after noon the bullets started dancing all around me — musket fire aimed directly at my flag and me. I was terrified but what could I do? I couldn't let our standard down and I certainly couldn't run off and leave my men in the lurch. So I just stood there while they launched six separate attacks against my flag.

"Oh, did I ever wish I had a gun," she said. "The men could at least fight back."

"I can't believe you're really here," Annie said.

Kady chuckled. "I feel the same way. When the enemy moved their heavy guns up, there were only a few of us left. We had no choice but to run for our lives."

Her smile faded as she sighed and fell silent.

"Then what?" Annie asked.

Kady shook her head. "It's hard even to talk about it. A man I never saw before, a Pennsylvanian, grabbed me and dragged me back into a thicket. We were hardly there when a shell came over and blew him to bits."

Annie caught her breath hard. It was clear from Kady's expression that the man had died there against her in that thicket. After a moment Kady raised her shoulders and let them drop heavily. "No more of that. I got away, and so did my husband. That's what *really* matters."

As Annie nodded, Kady's small square face twisted with sudden bitterness. "What upset me the most, even more than the bullets and the blood and all those men dying, was that people came to watch as if it were all a show."

"To watch?" Annie asked. "You mean the reporters and photographers?"

Kady shook her head angrily. "At least *they* were there on their business. I mean those Washington socialites. Can you believe those people?

They had driven out from the city in their fancy carriages to watch men die. They pitched fancy tents on the heights of the Potomac. Imagine, women in big brimmed hats and billowing muslin skirts. They'd brought picnics in fancy wicker baskets and sat under the trees eating fried chicken and sandwiches with their men. All this while we were fighting for our lives and losing a lot of them."

As she got more angry, Kady tugged more furiously at her tangled hair. Annie took the comb from her hand and worked at trying to straighten out the girl's long black hair. "Washington has always been thought of as a Southern city," she reminded Kady.

Kady twisted to stare at her, then nodded. "Not for long, Annie Etheridge," she said almost as if it were Annie that she was mad at. "In the end this will be an *American* city, just you wait and see."

Annie handed her comb back. "Forever," she said.

Kady ran her fingers through her shining hair. "Thanks for this, Annie, and for cheering me up, too!"

Annie rose. "Thank *you*, Kady. I feel brand-new."

Late that afternoon, Frank Thompson caught up with Annie. She had never seen him so excited. He caught her hands in his, his eyes shining. "Have you heard the news?" he asked. "Mrs. Hinsdale made it back."

Annie cried out with relief. "How wonderful," she said. "Is she all right?"

"She was pretty worn out from walking all the way from Manassas to Alexandria on foot. But the Rebels had caught her all right. They put her to work in their hospital in Manassas, but she somehow managed to get to General Beauregard. He signed a permission for her to come back to her own side."

Then he laughed. "The general must not have been thinking very clearly."

"Why do you say that?"

He grinned at Annie. "He didn't even make her sign a parole of honor."

Annie frowned. "I guess I don't know what that means."

"Well, you better learn if you're going to run around up in the front lines the way you do. A parole of honor is a signed promise on your honor that you won't report what you've seen or heard behind enemy lines."

"Oh, Jane Hinsdale would never sign such a thing as that," Annie said.

"You can get thrown into prison for refusing. But the general didn't even ask her to sign one. When she dragged in here, she marched straight up to Israel Richardson with lots of detailed information about the enemy's strength and positions. Think of that! She got to be a spy for the Union without even meaning to be."

"I just think it's great that she's safe," Annie said.

"I just think it would be great to carry news like that," Frank said. "It makes me jealous as all get out. This city is just jam-packed with Southern spies. We really need some cracking good ones of our own."

"What makes you so sure the South has spies here?"

He laughed that easy way, his head thrown back and his teeth gleaming. "Come on, Annie. How could General Beauregard have known where we were headed if some spy hadn't reported our plans?"

A shiver stirred up Annie's spine to think of enemy eyes watching their movements, counting their troops.

"Spying's a big part of war," Frank went on. "For myself, I'd rather be a spy than anything."

Annie grinned to herself. Frank was like a big excited kid. "They don't even wait for dawn to shoot spies," she reminded him.

He shrugged. "A bullet is a bullet in my book."

Five days after the bloody defeat at Bull Run, Major General George B. McClellan was brought from his successful campaigns in West Virginia and ordered to whip the Army of the Potomac into fighting trim. Annie was assigned to hospital duty in Alexandria while her regiment went back into training.

Twelve

Fall 1861 – Spring 1862

THE MANSION HOUSE HOSPITAL in Alexandria
was the ugliest building Annie had ever seen.
Annie pushed her way in through a mob on the
sidewalk. It was a madhouse inside, too, with
medical people running in all directions. The
building looked like a hotel, with a broad corridor
down its center and doors opening onto it every
few feet. Annie swallowed to keep from choking.
The stench of blood and pus was overpowering.
From the crannies along the hall came the groans
and cries of wounded men.

"Set your trunk down anywhere," an aide
ordered. "Be quick about it. There's work to do."

The next few days blurred into a haze of

exhaustion. The stream of wounded and disabled never stopped. Annie only reacted to a barked order here and an angry shout there. The small rooms were so crowded that she couldn't pass between the cots without shaking the wounded, making them groan.

By the third day she'd had enough of the way the ward was being run. The men lay silent, watching her as if she came from a different world. What did the hospital supervisors think they were doing? These weren't lumps of clay in the cots crammed into that stinking space. They were men — more like boys really.

So there weren't enough hands. Did that mean they couldn't try to bring some life into the wards? Her anger rose steadily. She hated the smells and the miserable food. She hated sleeping sitting up in a room. But more than anything she hated the way the patients were treated. If anyone ever treated her like that, she would either throw a grand tantrum or just curl up and die.

She decided to run her ward her own way no matter who got mad at her. She would ignore the shouts of "Come here," and "Hurry up." What law said you couldn't be friendly while you took a man's pulse or applied a poultice? *What would a few minutes matter by day's end?*

She started with a soldier who looked no older

than herself. As she took his pulse, she spoke to him. "You could give me a smile," she suggested, grinning herself. "It might make you feel better."

He stared at her. "I thought you only gave orders."

"I take orders, too," she told him. "I'm Annie," she added. "I like knowing people's names. What's yours?"

"Hal," he told her. "Not Private Porter, just Hal."

"Why do you look so glum, Hal?" she asked.

He shrugged. "I worry about my folks and my girl. They don't know what's happened to me."

"We can fix that," she said. "How about I bring you a pen and paper to write home?"

When he frowned, Annie felt awful. She had forgotten that a lot of boys had never been taught to write.

"Or," she went on, "I could write home for you."

His smile was blinding. "Would you really?"

She put his arm down and wrote his pulse on his chart. "You be thinking what to say. I'll be back after dinner."

The drum beat for dinner at twelve. The men who could walk went to the mess hall. Annie's job was to feed the others from trays. That day everyone wanted to talk.

"What did Hal do to make him your pet?" a

curly-headed Scotsman asked crossly between spoons of soup.

"What makes you think Hal's my pet?" she asked.

"You use his name and he claims you're writing a letter for him."

She wiped the soup off his mustache. "Well, he told me his name and I offered to write his letter."

"I'm Bruce and I'd like a letter, too," he said, as if daring her to refuse him.

"I forgot to say that Hal smiled at me, too," Annie told him, rising and setting his tray aside. "Practice smiling and think what to say and you're next after Hal, Bruce."

"Thanks, Annie," he growled, turning away to hide the twinkle in his eyes. Over those weeks, more and more men asked her help with letters. In a strange way, those letters were the hardest part of her days. How many times could you feel your heart break and still keep going?

"Homesickness is catching," she told herself as she carefully transcribed the stumbling words. Because their words and thoughts were so private, they spoke softly lest the other men hear them.

"Oh, what I wouldn't give to come up that path to home," a young sergeant whispered. "My heart lumps up past breathing just to think on

100

it. You'd come running down the path with your hair yellow in the sun and Shep at your heels, and I'd be like to cry, man that I am."

Annie caught her breath with pain. She was "like to cry" herself at his words. Had he forgotten that even when those bandages came off he would never see anything again? Not his Betty nor her dog nor any sunshine.

"Can you finish with something about her taking care of herself and the baby?" he asked, choked with emotion. "And love, and God's blessing?"

"I can do that," Annie told him, trying to keep tears from her voice.

She had no room of her own, but slept by propping a pillow against her trunk. She often lay there a long time with helpless tears trickling down her cheeks. Her arms ached from lifting men's heads to drink, from turning them in their beds, from bracing them on their first uncertain steps. Her stomach still churned from replacing the blood-drenched dressings of the amputees.

But it wasn't the pain of her body that brought the tears. It was longing. She wanted to dress up again the way she had the night of the dance. She wanted blackberry pie with the juice running red on the plate and home-churned ice cream melting on top. She tried to remember how it felt to lie between fragrant sheets and to go back to sleep again even when the morning sun streamed through the window.

Sometimes she raged with self-pity. No other girl whom she knew was as miserable as she was. Even if she left the army, where could she go? Not back to the Hammer house, remembering how Sophie's mother felt about her joining the regiment. Not back to Wisconsin, which had sad enough memories of its own. She was in a dreadful awful place with her life passing her by and nobody even cared!

As the stream of wounded patients lessened, the hospital became more orderly. The nurses settled down to a regular six-day work week that began with reveille at five in the morning and ended with the final bugle call at nine, when the lights went out and the talk in the wards had to stop.

After she broke the ice with Hal and Bruce, Annie's ward changed. Soon she knew every man's name and had written letters for many of them. At first, when the night bugle sounded, only a few men called, "Good night, Annie" as she set out the medicine for the night watchers. By the end of the second week, the greeting came from every bed in the crowded room.

The weeks passed and the months. Annie sometimes spent her one day off a week with Will Hammer. He was with the rest of the regiment, which was being drilled night and day by the new commanding officer, General McClellan. Will looked lean and trim from the hard exercise but his spirits were good.

He often brought news from home and took her to eat in restaurants with linen on the tables and fresh flowers. Not all his news was good. He told of Belle's death, off in Grand Rapids with her sister. He told her that Edwin Powers had broken his pledge to Sophie and enlisted.

"Sophie will forgive him, won't she?" Annie asked. "She *has* to understand."

He shrugged. "Who knows about Sophie?"

He changed the subject quickly to go back to safe army talk. "This McClellan isn't much taller than a drummer boy. The men all call him Little Mac. But he's a wonder, Annie. He's whipping this army into winning shape. And we even like him for it."

December came with snow frosting the tree limbs outside Annie's window. By the time the buds began to swell, she was completely caught up in the hospital routine.

In the mornings after the men had made up their beds and washed, they had breakfast at six o'clock. The end of this meal began Annie's favorite part of the hospital day. The men felt their best and their spirits were high. After the room was cleaned, they relaxed, joked with each other, and chose their own entertainments.

The happy ones packed their bags to rejoin their regiments or return home. Others read, played checkers, or dreamed while they waited for the surgeon to make his daily rounds.

Hal was packing to leave on a March morning. He was smiling so broadly that Annie teased him. "I never saw anyone so glad to go back to the farm," she told him. "Are you really that crazy about slopping pigs?"

He flushed. "I'm marrying my Molly," he said quietly.

"Why are you whispering?" she asked him. "Wouldn't these fellows like to hear some *good* news for a change?"

He blushed again, "They might," he agreed. "Tell."

Annie went to the middle of the room and clapped her hands. All eyes turned to her. "Hal has a word to say," she told them.

Hal stumbled his announcement out with a flaming face. When he finished, Bruce called out, "Let's hear it for Hal and his Molly!"

Just as the ward exploded with cheers, the fife and drums announced the arrival of the surgeon. Annie's heart plunged. She crossed her fingers hoping this would be one of the surgeons who didn't hate having women in hospitals.

Then he was there, the surgeon himself with

his assistants wide-eyed behind him. A short, broad man with white chop whiskers, he had eyes like the points of two bayonets. "What is the meaning of this?" he thundered.

The ward fell silent under his glaring eyes. Then he fixed on Annie. She nodded the way Belle had taught her.

"The men are cheering the joy of one of their friends," she said quietly, having some trouble getting the words out.

"Young woman," he said. "This is a hospital, not a sporting event." He turned to his assistants. "From the beginning it has been a dire mistake to permit women in the medical service. They are a nuisance, a disturbing influence, and a distraction to the well-being of our men."

At this the men began to grumble, a grumble that rose to a shout that filled the hall outside with curious people. Annie's name was heard over and over. The surgeon's face reddened with fury as he turned to her. "Madam," he said, his voice trembling with anger. "Leave this ward. And be warned! I'm reporting you."

As Annie stood, scarlet with embarrassment, the men began to laugh. They knew, if the surgeon didn't, that only her regiment's general had any authority over her. Annie gasped. If he had been that upset about the men's cheering, he would be completely destroyed by their laugh-

105

ing at him. She slipped out into the hall to escape.

She hadn't taken three steps before a strong arm caught her. "General Richardson," she gasped. He was carrying his straw hat and grinning as he used to back in Detroit. His free hand was in his pocket, just like old times.

"At your service, Annie." He laughed. "I was here to see some of our people and you were on my list."

Annie caught her breath. What would he say when he learned that she had gotten into so much trouble? "We need you back," he went on. "The men won't talk about going on the spring campaign without 'gentle Annie.' "

"Today?" she asked breathlessly, hardly able to believe her good luck. "Can I come with you today?"

He laughed. "Always the little soldier! You can ride back with me, unless the hospital needs you a few days more."

"I assure you, they won't mind at all," she told him.

She backed away, smiling. Maybe later she would explain. She might even *have* to explain if the surgeon put her on report. For now she only wanted to get her trunk and escape.

When she got back, she saw the surgeon down the corridor. She crept into her wardroom, signaling for silence. "I came to tell you good-bye," she whispered. "General Richardson has called me back to the regiment." They began to protest, but Bruce growled at them.

"Do you guys want Annie's head on a tray? Good luck, girl, and our thanks." She fought tears at the low rumble of "Thanks, Annie." She threw them a kiss and fled.

Thirteen

March – April 1862

ANNIE'S REGIMENT went back into action that
spring with a new flag. The silk flag that Annie
loved had been riddled by bullets and returned
to the women who had made it.

On March seventeenth, the Army of the Potomac, one-hundred-and-twenty-thousand-men
strong, massed at the piers of Alexandria. The
green hills were plastered with horses and men
and shining weaponry. Flags sprouted above a
sea of men in blue. Annie could hardly keep her
feet still as the regimental bands filled the warm
air with stirring music.

Every possible kind of boat crowded the Potomac River — transatlantic packets, three-

decked steamers, barges, flat bottoms, even canal boats. As the four hundred vessels were unmoored, Annie looked back at Washington. Although the dome was unfinished, the Capitol rose gleaming above the trees.

"Any idea where we're going?" Frank asked her. From his grin, she was sure that he already knew.

"Only that it's a long way," she told him.

"How do you figure that?"

"There are too many supplies for just a short journey."

He shook his head. "See? I keep telling you. You're being wasted carrying that pillbox. You'd be a great spy."

She said nothing. Once she would have said she would settle for being a great nurse. She wasn't sure anymore. There was too much heartbreak in nursing. She still grieved that Fred Wustenberg had lost the arm she treated at Bull Run. She had done all she could and still could not save it.

She stared at the restless water. What *would* she like to do more than anything else? The answer was too simple, and not helpful at all. She'd like to be a girl again, clean and fragrant, and with people she loved. She'd like to laugh and dance and have wonderful hot food on beautiful plates.

"From the look on your face, you must be thinking of something pretty wonderful," Frank said, studying her.

She chuckled. "I am. And believe me, Frank. It's not spying in a bloody, dirty war, and sleeping in a tent."

Their boat entered Chesapeake Bay on the second day. The Virginia shore was a shadowy silhouette on the horizon, mysterious and threatening. As the ship passed Hampton Road, clouds boiled up into a storm. Giant waves crashed against the boat, plunging it from side to side.

One of the soldiers, green with seasickness, staggered from the rail to Annie's side. "If I get to land alive," he gasped, "not even an army will get me out on water again."

Annie didn't argue. Solid land sounded pretty good to her, too. The billows slammed the vessels against each other, threatening the lives of the hundreds of men crowding the ships. Even when the boats were moored, the waves broke some of their cables, sending them drifting out of control.

But land was no better. They marched to Hampton leaning into a wind that hammered them with rain. Vivid lightning split the sky and the trees whipped like tortured phantoms.

The general didn't arrive until the second of April. Annie was so sick of shivering in a dark, wet tent that she didn't even mind setting off on another march. She did wish for a horse. Her boots grew heavier with every step.

Frank called this march the first move in the Peninsular Campaign. "Think about the map of Virginia," he told her. "A big chunk of land lies between the York and the James rivers. The Confederate capitol at Richmond lies at the west end of that peninsula."

"And we mean to capture it?" Annie asked.

"We are *going* to capture it," Frank corrected her.

Annie wanted to lash out at him. She didn't need a geography lesson, she needed a discharge. Her wet clothes scraped her skin. Her empty stomach growled and her legs ached. *She* didn't want any part of Virginia, much less the city of Richmond. She wanted *out*. She would ask for a discharge, that's what she would do! The minute they got back to some decent place, she'd just pack her trunk and go!

She was still having a private silent tantrum when the event happened that made her forget even the layers of mud on her boots. There, on that miserable road to Yorktown, General Philip Kearney appeared. He was so different, so daring, and so fascinating that she forgot herself for the fun of seeing him in action.

They were crawling along behind a supply train. They could neither speed up nor pass the covered wagons reeling and pitching in the sucking yellow mud. When Annie thought things

111

could get no worse, she heard rifle fire up ahead. She gasped. They couldn't even defend themselves if the Confederates launched an attack. Stuck on that miserable road they were all sitting ducks for enemy fire.

Then she heard thundering hoofbeats behind her. She turned to see a massive white horse charging up from the rear. She and the men scattered to one side and watched the officer speed by. Two mounted men followed hard on the officer's heels, spraying thick mud.

A few yards farther on, the officer wheeled, rearing his horse. Annie barely caught his shouted words over the crackling rifle fire. He was literally roaring. He ordered his men to arrest the guards of the wagon train. "At once," he shouted. "Every man Jack of them."

One guard made the mistake of protesting but the general drowned him out. "Tip those wagons off the road or I'll burn them where they stand," he stormed. "My division was ordered here to fight and *I will have this road.*"

Against the background of the increasing rifle fire, the wagons were shoved aside. When the officer turned, Annie noticed that his left sleeve was empty.

Annie stared at him in wonder. This was how a general *should* look! He was large, broad-shouldered, with a strong-featured face and a handsome drooping mustache. Even in the rain, his uniform looked immaculate. Straight in the saddle with his sword at his side, he motioned his men forward. A bright red patch shone on his hat. His men streamed by, all wearing the same red diamond patch — officers on their hats, enlisted men on their sleeves up near the shoulder.

He had barely wheeled and ordered his men forward before the woods shuddered with volley after volley of gunfire. The engagement was brief. Within minutes the enemy rifles fell silent and the columns moved forward. As they passed the ditched supply train, Annie grinned crazily to herself.

"I liked that," she said to no one in particular. "I mean, I really *liked* that!"

The corporal marching on Annie's left looked over at her. "The only folks that don't like Kearney are the Rebels. Those Confederate pickets won't try sneaking up on *that* general again. He puts on quite a show, doesn't he?"

"Wonderful," Annie said, craning to try to see the mounted figure on the white horse again. "Who is he? I don't remember ever seeing him before."

"You'll see a lot more of him before this is through," he told her. "That's General Philip Kearney. He's been called the perfect soldier by better men than you and me."

Then she remembered the missing arm. Fred

Wustenberg got an honorable discharge after his arm was amputated. She didn't mean to say it out loud, but the words just popped out. "With only one arm?" she asked.

He shrugged, still grinning. "That's old apples to Kearney. He lost that left arm when he was a young man down in Mexico. He told somebody he would give an arm to lead a cavalry charge. He led one and paid the price."

"And it's never bothered him?"

"Not that he's mentioned." The man laughed. "His aide says he jokes that it makes it tough to get a glove on. After Mexico he fought for the French in Algiers and again in northern Italy. Won a lot of medals even."

He showed Annie the patch on his own sleeve. "The Kearney patch," he said proudly. "It's for bravery. Aren't you with Richardson's Second Michigan?"

At Annie's nod, he continued. "Your regiment will get to wear it, too. You've been assigned to Kearney's Division."

His words made Annie's heart sing. Oh, to wear that red diamond patch! To be back in battle and *win!* She was sick of withdrawals and retreats or whatever they wanted to call it when they lost a battle. She couldn't imagine General Philip Kearney ever calling retreat.

On the fifth day of marching, they reached the Warwick River. According to Annie's companions, this sluggish stream would only slow their march to Yorktown. They were half right. The Warwick didn't slow the march. It stopped it. The fortifications that the Confederate Army had built along the river ground the Federal advance to a stop. The one bright thing in those dark days was the red patch Annie was given.

For nearly a month, all Annie fought was malaria. A field hospital was hastily constructed for the sick and dying. Annie was used to nursing wounded men but these soldiers were *sick*! Those who survived were taken from the field to the Transport Service on the river. To Annie's dismay, she was assigned to go with them in a slow-moving covered wagon humming with insects.

The wagon finally emerged from the woods. Annie hadn't seen so many boats since leaving Alexandria. As the carts stopped, the small boat that came to nudge at the edge of the wharf looked like a well-worn tugboat. On its deck stood three young girls, waving and smiling. They wore plain brown aprons over their straight skirts. No crinolines!

The tallest girl was the first up the rope ladder. "So you're the famous Annie Etheridge," she said, grabbing Annie's hand. "Welcome aboard the *Wicked Chicken*."

They swiftly got the patients aboard. Within minutes the boat pushed off into the dark Virginia night.

Fourteen
April – May 6, 1862

THE TRUE NAME of the tugboat was *Wissahickon*. The girls had covered the floor of the small shelter cabin with straw mattresses to be ready for the patients. The boat would have held twenty-five men comfortably. By the time they finished loading her that night, they had managed to fit fifty of the stricken men aboard.

"First get something for them to drink," one of the girls told Annie. "Sick men are always thirsty first thing."

"Water?" Annie asked, looking around for a bucket.

The girl shook her head. "The river water is too muddy to drink," she said. "There's some rainwater in the galley." She nodded toward the

116

stairs. "We don't have lemons but vinegar with molasses is *almost* like lemonade."

Before Annie got the mixture made, the tug began to move. She braced herself as she moved from patient to patient, holding the tin cup to each man's lips. They drank thirstily, careful to get the very last drop of the strange-smelling liquid.

Someone had set water to boil and brewed tea in a giant stockpot. This they handed around with chunks of bread slathered with more of the molasses. Once fed, the patients grew quieter. Up on the deck Annie watched the banks of the river slide by in the darkness. "We didn't give you much of a welcome," the girl with the nice smile said, joining Annie. "But that's how it is when we pick up patients." She shook Annie's hand. "Welcome aboard. I'm Amy."

Annie smiled. "Where are we taking them?" she asked.

"Down the river to a bigger boat," Amy explained, leaning her elbows on the rail. "We haven't been doing this very long. We're just lucky that the Sanitary Commission was able to get hospital ships and permission to establish the Hospital Transport Service. The whole thing was a mess before we started."

"You have real ocean-going ships?" Annie asked, remembering her nervous trip through the Chesapeake Bay.

117

Amy nodded. "Wait'll you see the *Daniel Webster*. She carried two hundred and fifty sick men to a New York hospital and got back nine days later. Now that's a turnaround." When one of the men cried out, both girls turned. Amy nodded at Annie. "Let me go. You need to put on one of our stylish brown aprons before you really get in the swing." She checked the man then went to get him medicine.

At dawn they reached the river's mouth and transferred the patients to the hospital ship. The girls scrambled back onto the *"Wicked Chicken,"* which was ready to plug upstream.

During the weeks and finally months she served with the Hospital Transport Service, Annie watched the organization grow and expand and perform large miracles with their tiny water-spider boats.

The girls were as wonderful as they were different. All were kind to the soldiers in their own way. They jested with the ailing boys to draw smiles from them. One of the shyest of the girls had a sweet clear voice that soothed pain better than any medicine. When she sang "Auld Lang Syne" or "Home, Sweet Home," the men on the cots fell silent, forgetting their pain in thoughts of home.

The *Wilson Small* was Annie's favorite of all the boats. Space was so tight on it that when it was filled with patients, she and the other girls slept on straw sacks leaning against a wall. Having no table, nor a place to put one, they used a board supported on the stairs to eat from.

On the Pamunkey River, Annie first saw the famous Union supply base called White House. Here were stored the vast number of supplies needed by the Army of the Potomac.

"It has to be big," Amy reminded her. "We are simply out here with enemies in front of us and enemies in back. What chance would long wagon trains have of getting through to us?"

Rumors were constant about the siege on the Warwick River. When word came that the Confederate Army had slipped away in the night, Annie refused to believe it. "Our army is chasing them," one of the pilots said. "When they catch up, we'll have our hands full."

All day on the fifth of May the sound of gunfire boomed along the river. The *Wilson Small* turned her prow toward the clouds of smoke rising above the forest. It was raining. When the *Wilson Small* reached the beach, the battle was over. What was left of Annie's army was marching in triumph down the streets of the ancient city of Williamsburg.

Once the wounded began to be brought on board, no one had time to think. All that day and the next, the little tug scuttled back and forth, delivering the wounded to hospital ships. The sun broke through in late afternoon on the second day. As it set, a fresh load of patients was carried onto the boat. As Annie braced a stretcher-bearer coming on board, she looked down the river and shuddered. The sunset colors had stained the muddy surface of the river to the same deep shade as the dried blood on her sleeves and skirt.

When a soldier with a chest wound groaned, she leaned over him. He was barely conscious and lay with his head turned away. His bandage, which had clearly been applied some time earlier, was hardening as his blood dried. She went for a basin of warm water. Working as carefully as she could, she tried to soak the cloth away from his flesh without starting the bleeding again.

He twisted under her hands with a little cry.

"I'll try not to hurt you," she told him. "As soon as this is cleaned, I'll bring you something for the pain."

She felt his eyes on her face and tried to smile without endangering the delicate process of peeling the dressing back. The weakness in his voice didn't surprise her, given his loss of blood. The teasing banter in his words caught her off guard.

"How about a gallon of cider and a dozen ginger cookies?" he asked quietly, keeping his eyes on hers.

She stared at him, startled. At first she didn't recognize Edwin Powers. Back in Detroit with Sophie he had been clean-shaven with his eyes bright in a fair-skinned face. *This* Edwin Powers had a heavy auburn beard and his face was deeply tanned. But there was no mistaking his voice.

"Edwin," she cried. "What can I say? I haven't had time even to look at my patients today." She started to add how good it was to see him but caught her words in time. It *wasn't* good to see him like this — weak and exhausted with that horrible wound in his chest.

He shook his head slightly. "I'm lucky to get you. I guess you heard that I waited a bit and joined another outfit," he paused. "Couldn't tear myself away from Sophie and home."

His words echoed in her mind. Sophie and home.

"I did see Will back there during the siege," he said after a minute. "How he brags on you!"

As he spoke, she finally released the clotted bandage to reveal his wound. She steeled herself to conceal her sudden anguish. Half of Edwin's pale chest had been torn away, exposing part of the slow tortuous beating of his heart. She forced herself to smile at him. "I could do my bragging on Will if we had time," she told him. "We're *old* friends."

When he caught her hand, she knew she had failed to hide her shock from him. His blue eyes were no longer smiling but icy. "How much time for me, Annie?" he asked quietly.

"Edwin, I'm not a doctor."

"I didn't ask a doctor. I asked you how much time."

She hesitated, unable to meet his gaze. If he had the best possible surgeon in the best possible hospital, could he even make it then? But he would have neither of these. He would be shunted off this boat on a stretcher and onto another. So many injured had poured out of Williamsburg onto that beach, that it would be a miracle if he managed to get onto a surgically equipped ship to go north.

"It's a very serious wound," she told him quietly.

He nodded only the least bit. "I think I knew that."

"But you're not to give up hope, Edwin. Hear me?"

He had turned his face away. "I hear, Annie," he said quietly. "Could you hold my hand a minute and let me pretend that you're Sophie?"

Amy, across the room, knitted her brows and looked at Annie with a question in her face. Maybe she saw Annie's tears. In any case she turned back to her patient with the friendly chatter that made her such a comforting nurse. "We're almost there, fellows," she said. "I can tell by the way this tub feels that we're turning in. Hang on. Better help is on the way. You

122

might even get beef tea on the big ship. Those doctors are really into beef tea."

Then the first of the stretcher-bearers entered to start moving the men out.

"You'll be on the hospital ship right away," Annie told Edwin. "Hold yourself as stiffly as you can so as not to start that bleeding again."

He didn't seem to have heard her. "Tell Sophie I have loved her always, Annie," he whispered. "And I always will."

She wanted to cry out to him, to take him bodily in hand and force him to live. But he was slipping away from her by the second. His hand released hers and dropped heavily to his side. "I love her," he gasped.

Annie seized his arm and felt for the pulse she already knew wasn't there. When she stumbled to her feet, Amy caught her hand and led her out on deck. "You knew him from home?" she asked.

Amy's voice seemed to come from a great hollow distance. Annie heard the words echoing in her mind, "from home — from home" and nodded silently.

Amy kept talking in a low, comforting tone but Annie heard no more. She felt the pressure of Amy's arms around her but began to shiver with an icy cold. Across the black hollowness that filled Annie she faintly heard Amy's warning,

"Watch out, we're coming alongside."

It was strange, as if Annie were standing alone in a place she didn't recognize. Waves of grief brought silent tears coursing from her eyes. Her mind cried out to Sophie, who was beyond the reach of her voice, and to Edwin, beyond the reach of all voices.

A stretcher-bearer jarred against her as he tried to maneuver through the narrow door. Annie stared at him dully, watching him pass as if he were a creature from another world. When the last three stretchers were carried out, the faces of the men were covered.

Her eyes flew open and she stifled a cry. Edwin. One of them had to be Edwin.

She turned and groped her way back into the boat, blinded by her tears. Dully, she decided that the water had somehow turned restless. She couldn't see clearly and everything whirled before her eyes. As she caught at the wall for support, she heard a high, shrill cry that could have been her own, then nothing.

Fifteen

May 7 – July 4, 1862

ANNIE WAKENED to an easy rocking rhythm. She was warmly wrapped in a nest of blankets with her clothes loosened and her hair let down. Where was she? How had she come here? What had happened? Only when she heard the murmur of women's voices from above and the pulse of the ship's engine, did the black wave of memory bring her upright.

Edwin!

She pressed her hands against her face to shut away the images of his naked, pounding heart, his face covered in death. She rocked back and forth with her eyes closed. She couldn't bear it — not anymore. Never again, not ever ever again could she do this. Home. Somehow she had to get home. She hadn't realized that she'd said the word *home* aloud until Amy spoke from the door.

"Good! You're awake," she said softly. "I brought tea."

Annie stared at her, feeling hot tears running heedlessly down her face. "What happened?" she finally asked when Amy had pressed the cup into her hands.

"I guess you fainted," Amy said. "No wonder."

"It was Edwin," Annie whispered, just as if the name would mean something to Amy. "Edwin Powers. He was engaged to my best friend."

"But you were there with him," Amy reminded her. "How much worse it might have been."

Her words inflamed Annie with an unreasonable anger. "How much worse! Don't even say that. There is *nothing* worse than this dreadful brutal war, nothing ever, anywhere. The pain, the blood, the waste of lives!"

Amy nodded soberly, staring at her hands in her lap. "I won't argue that."

"I'm through," Annie said, not even caring that she was almost shouting. "I can't stand any more of it. I won't."

"I know how you feel," Amy replied.

"You can't know how I feel," Annie raged at her. "You're still here, aren't you?"

Amy's smile was strange and crooked. "Only because even if I went away, I couldn't forget it. This way I can do something about it."

126

Annie stared into her cup. Something, she thought, but never enough. Then suddenly Sophie was full in her mind — happy, carefree Sophie. Her tears started afresh. "She doesn't even know," Annie wailed. "Sophie doesn't even know about Edwin." How could she write such words to her dear friend, when she couldn't endure the thought herself?

"Drink your tea," Amy told her. "And be thankful you could do what you did."

Annie looked up at her, startled, but Amy had risen and left her alone. "It will never be the same again," Annie whispered aloud to the empty cabin. "Never the same."

Annie's strength was slow to return. Sometimes without warning she remembered Edwin's hand on hers and wept. More than anything she wished she could talk to Will. But he was in the field with the regiment and she was on the river.

Late in May, General McClellan launched a new campaign that lasted for two months. On the first of July, the army had abandoned the base at White House and Annie joined her regiment at Harrison's Landing.

She fought back tears when she finally saw her old friends again. Will, gaunt from malaria, listened silently as Annie told him of Edwin's death. "I'll write Sophie at once," he promised. "The army has certainly notified his parents, but his last words will mean everything to Sophie."

She was almost afraid to ask him if Sophie had made peace with Edwin over his enlistment. He smiled at her. "Did you ever know Sophie to hold a grudge for ten minutes?"

He patted her shoulder awkwardly, then changed the subject. "What's your friend Frank Thompson been up to? He wasn't with us in this campaign and yet he turned up here at the landing as soon as we got here."

"Maybe you just missed him," Annie suggested.

He shook his head. "I went looking for him, hoping to get news of you. Nobody seemed to know where he was."

Annie shrugged but felt a little ripple of excitement. Had Frank's fondest dream finally come true? Had he been relieved from the regiment to spy for the Union Army?

"Whatever it is, he'll probably tell you," Will said. "That guy really likes to talk."

Frank turned up at Annie's tent without warning. "How's my favorite nurse?" he called through the flap.

She almost called back to ask how her favorite spy was, but caught herself in time. But one look at his face confirmed her guess. He *couldn't* look that happy about anything else. He barely greeted her before spilling out his stories about spy missions into enemy territory. She didn't know how much to believe, but his tales were wonderful.

"You could be a famous gossip," she told him, remembering Will's words.

He looked at her strangely, then laughed. "A spy is just a gossip with a cause," he said. "Would you believe me if I said that President Lincoln is coming here?

"Well, he is," Frank insisted when she grinned at him.

Annie shook her head. "Why should he come all the way down here through enemy territory?"

"To review his troops," Frank said. Then he shrugged. "He might even want to change generals again, seeing that we still haven't won a major battle, much less the war."

Something about his tone made her halfway believe him, and the hope made her tremble. "You better be right about this rumor," she warned him, "or I'll never forgive you."

"Why is it so important to you?" he asked.

Annie couldn't put into words why seeing President Abraham Lincoln was almost too exciting to believe.

And of course Frank was right. The minute the rumor stiffened to fact, the area boiled with activity. Sailors crawled like ants over the gunboats, swabbing decks, polishing cannons, and clambering up and down the rigging. The drill sergeants barked at their men from dawn until sunset. A supply boat brought new uniforms for the men. Annie hardly recognized her friends in their spanking new blue outfits.

But wait! She was a part of this regiment, too. She couldn't disgrace them in front of the president! She passed the time by putting her battle-scarred riding habit into presentable condition.

Independence Day dawned clear and hot with sunlight mirrored on the restless river. Annie was too excited to eat. Finally the unbelievable happened. The drums rolled and the regimental bands began to play, stirring the leaves on what trees had survived the cannons of the gunboats.

The 2nd Michigan Volunteers were stationed more than halfway down the line. Annie stretched to stand tall as she took her place with the men. She was supposed to look straight ahead but she sneaked quick glances. How wonderful the lean, tanned men looked in their crisp new uniforms. When the president and General McClellan *finally* appeared, a whisper of excitement rustled through the troops like wind in tall corn. Annie found herself too excited to breathe.

She had read and heard about this man, Abraham Lincoln, as long as she could remember. She had heard him praised and blamed in equal measure. But her father had believed in him as the restless nation's best hope. He had become mythical to her, a human larger than life in all

130

respects. Certainly she had never expected to *see* him in the living flesh.

The president and the general rode side by side, reviewing the regiments in turn. General McClellan seemed shrunken beside his lanky companion. He sat as tight in his saddle as the president looked disjointed. The president's knees were cocked at an uncomfortable angle as if no stirrups could ever keep such legs from dragging the ground. As they passed each regiment, the president removed his stovepipe hat in salute. As the horses moved quickly, Annie studied this man. Much had been said about his immense height and leanness. "As thin as the rails he split as a boy," someone said. He looked to Annie like the bare bones of a man tumbled into a black frock coat whose sleeves were too short.

Much had been said about his humor and his simple homespun stories. This day he rode in silence, as the general at his side leaned toward him now and then to say something.

Nothing had been said about his face except that he was plain. She studied his features so intently that she ceased to hear the music. He was plain, astonishingly plain. But as he lifted his hat in front of her regiment Annie looked into his eyes. They were the saddest and gentlest eyes she had ever seen. Her excitement was

131

replaced by compassion. His dark eyes seemed to mourn the death of every soldier who had fallen on the fields of this war. She didn't see him pass on by for the hot tears burning behind her eyelids.

The conditions at Harrison's Landing improved after the president's visit, with the arrival of three hundred hospital tents. "You know this is too good to last," Frank warned Annie. "The Rebs have driven our army out of Manassas."

"But that's up by Centreville and Blackburn's Ford. That's where we started!" Annie protested.

"It's also a quick march from Washington for the Southerners," he reminded her. "I'll bet we'll be back up there to stop them in a matter of weeks."

Never had a base been dismantled so swiftly. When, on August fourteenth, Annie's regiment began the march toward Williamsburg, she sought out Frank. "What's happening?" he asked as she stood facing him with her hands on her hips.

"I just want you to know that I'm sick of your being right all the time."

He laughed. "Can I help it if I'm a better spy than Allan Pinkerton?" On August twenty-seventh, the regiment started back toward Centreville and Bull Run.

Sixteen

August – September 1862

ANNIE'S REGIMENT fought its way to Bull Run. The Confederate Cavalry attacked fiercely at Blackburn's Ford. After a swift and bloody battle, the enemy finally retreated. As they fell in to march to Centreville, Annie looked back at that level bottomland, those dark woods. "A year and a month ago," she said quietly.

"But we're none of us the same," the sergeant at her side said with a grin. "Last time we weren't wearing these." He touched Annie's shoulder and the red diamond Kearney patch on it that matched his own.

She nodded, as proud as any of them to be following General Kearney. But she was changed in more ways than this. Blackburn's Ford itself had made the war real for her. Here she first saw violent death, smelled gunpowder mingled with human blood, and knew, without the whisper of a doubt, that she was where she was supposed to be.

The army itself was much changed, with many old comrades fallen to disease or gunfire. Annie missed Kady Brownell who had returned to Rhode Island after her husband was wounded in action. As Annie stared at the bullet-scarred trees and the patches of grass blackened by shell fire, she was startled by music. She paused, listening intently to the full-throated singing of the 12th Massachusetts Regiment.

"What's that wonderful song they're singing?"

"Catchy, isn't it?" the sergeant agreed. "It's just an old hymn. It's called, 'Say, Brothers, Will We Meet You Over on the Other Shore?' "

"That's not what they are singing."

He nodded. "The Twelfth put their own words to the tune. It's all about the martyr John Brown."

Annie found herself marching and singing along with the others. The song was more than catchy, it was irresistible. *"John Brown's body lies amouldering in his grave, and we go marching on."*

The firing started early on the morning of the twenty-ninth but the day was nearly spent before

Kearney and Hooker's men were sent in. The battle lines changed swiftly with first one side and then the other seizing the advantage as men fell to a hail of murderous gunfire.

Annie, near the front line, was surrounded by the wounded and fallen who had no shelter from the exploding shells. She looked desperately for a way to help them.

She heard a groan and realized that it came from a rocky ledge that was studded with brush and thickets. Some of the wounded had already crawled in under its protection. Without noticing that her regiment had changed position, she helped or half-dragged several wounded men into this shelter so she could tend to their wounds. As she held a canteen of water to a young infantryman's lips, he smiled and spoke to her. Before his words were out, a shell from an enemy battery tore him to pieces under her hands.

She looked up in horror to realize that the Rebels were almost upon her. Gathering her skirts, she fled across the broken field to join her regiment.

As darkness fell she stayed on the field tending the fallen. She was startled when a horse was checked at her side, and a man's voice called her name. She groaned to herself. How many times had officers ordered her to the rear in battle when she was really needed up in the front lines?

She looked up into General Kearney's face, ready to give him an argument. But he wasn't like the others.

Instead of barking at her, his voice was warm with approval. "That's right," he told her. "I'm glad to see you here helping these poor fellows. From now on you will be a sergeant major, and I'll see to it that you have a horse of your own."

Annie tightened her arms against her sides lest she burst with happiness. To have Philip Kearney's approval was like a dream come true!

The battle raged all the next day, beginning at dawn and still thundering away until almost sunset. Late in the day the Confederate batteries felled so many of the Federal troops that General Lee captured several thousand prisoners.

The Union Army retreated behind the earthworks at Centreville. They had lost the Second Battle of Bull Run and their campaign to force Lee's retreat from Washington.

Late in the afternoon of September first, rain began to fall in torrents. The sky was vivid with lightning and pealing with such thunder that the guns of battle could not be heard three miles away.

The Union Cavalry, seeing the enemy circling to cut them off from the retreat to Washington, sent two generals, Kearney and Pope, off toward Washington with their troops.

The two forces clashed in a wild bloody fight

near a country house in Chantilly with the Confederate forces finally being repulsed.

During the fray General Kearney galloped through the dripping woods on his horse, Bayard. Carrying his sword in his hand and holding his reins in his teeth, he unwittingly charged behind enemy lines.

At the cry of "Halt," the general flattened himself on Bayard's back, sunk his spurs into his sides and made a dash for his own lines. At least half a dozen muskets rang out. Within a few yards he rolled dead from his horse's back onto the drenched earth.

Later Annie and the men of the 2nd Michigan Regiment learned that Kearney's dead body had been taken to a nearby farmhouse. The Confederate General A. P. Hill had gone there to pay his respects. Later, General Lee sent an ambulance through the lines under a white flag to deliver Kearney's body as a "consolation to his family." The horse, Bayard, and certain other of his possessions were returned to his widow.

Hardened soldiers that they were, Kearney's men stood and wept without shame even as Annie did.

"There never has been such a general," one of the men muttered.

"Nor will there be again," someone echoed.

The shadow that had fallen on Annie's heart with the death of Sophie's Edwin deepened into wordless grief that she couldn't even share with her comrades-in-arms.

Annie, with her new title and privileges, was detailed to brigade headquarters. For the following year she served as cook for the officer's mess. This didn't keep her from the front line of the battles (and defeats) that followed. There were so many battles and they followed so swiftly, one after another, that to name a battle was to bring a vivid quick scene to Annie's mind.

Frail mists had trailed through the valley at Antietam over endless fields of corn. Since no supplies had arrived, the doctors dressed the men's wounds with corn husks. One of the women, lacking instruments, removed a soldier's bullet with her buttonhole scissors. But at least two successful camp hospitals had been established to ease the suffering of the survivors.

Then there was the curious story that Frank Thompson told Annie when the guns of Antietam finally fell silent.

"There was great loss on that field," he told her.

She nodded. Didn't she know that, having worked among the dead and dying herself?

"A lot of soldiers had to be buried where they fell out there," he said. "I took pains to dig one grave myself."

She looked at him, puzzled. Why was he making such a point of something that wasn't new at all? Ever since First Bull Run, more than a year before, men had been buried where they fell if only to protect their bodies from the elements and the wheeling birds.

"This was a girl that I buried," Frank said slowly.

Annie looked up at him, startled, trying to think what girl had been on that field besides herself.

He nodded. "Just as truly a girl as you are, Annie Etheridge. Young she was, but somehow she had been made a corporal. Her hands were thick with calluses from carrying a rifle all this time. She had passed for a soldier all this time, she had."

"You are saying that to shock me," she told him.

"You have your way to fight this war. She had hers," he said, smiling in a way that Annie didn't really understand.

The other memorable event that followed the Battle at Antietam created a great stir throughout the entire nation, both North and South. President Lincoln issued the Emancipation Proclamation, freeing all the slaves.

Seventeen

December 1862 – May 1863

ONLY AFTER THE BATTLE at Fredericksburg did the regiment finally retire to winter camp. Philip Kearney's death had bound the members of the Red Diamond Division as close as brothers. Often Annie, wrapped in a buffalo robe against the winter chill, joined the men over evening camp-fires, listening to their endless stories, humming as they sang. In February, to one such dying campfire, a cavalryman brought the new words for that brisk infectious melody Annie had first heard at Bull Run.

"Hey, fellows," he said. "Any of you heard the new words to 'John Brown's Body'?"

When no one spoke up, he began to sing:
"Mine eyes have seen the glory of the coming of the

Lord. *He has trampled out the vintage where the grapes of wrath are stored. He has loosed the fateful lightning of his terrible swift sword. His truth goes marching on."*

At first the men only hummed the melody. Once he sang the chorus, their voices swelled in with the words, *"Glory, glory, Hallelujah. His truth goes marching on."*

Annie's heart thundered with the rightness of the words, and some of the men cheered.

"Where did *those* words come from?" one of the men asked. "Who wrote them?"

"Some poet named Julia Ward Howe," the man who had started the song replied. "They say she made them up in a Washington hotel room after hearing our own Michigan Black Hat Brigade march to the old words. Something else, ain't they?"

"Something else," Annie echoed.

That same month Frank brought Annie another of his surprises. "Have you ever hungered to see the Mississippi River?" he asked her, grinning.

"Not that I can remember," she admitted.

"You may get a chance. The rumor is that the Second Michigan will be sent to the Western Army come spring."

"I wish I didn't believe you," she said. "But those rumors of yours tend to turn into fact. When do we leave?"

He laughed. "I didn't say anything was going

to happen. I just said there was a rumor."

Of course the rumor was right. Frank told Annie good-bye before the regiment left for Newport News and the Kentucky front. The unexpected news was that Annie wasn't to go with them. Instead, she had been transferred to the 3rd Michigan to stay with the Army of the Potomac.

"I'm going to miss you like thunder, Annie Etheridge," Frank said, grinning at her. "You've been like a sister."

Annie made herself laugh. She *would* miss Frank dreadfully after all this time. "And you've been like a brother," she said, thinking of Will Hammer. "A frightful tease but fun for all of that!"

In Detroit, spring meant robins fussing in the apple tree. In the army, spring meant marching back into battle. Annie had learned how to pack from the girls in the Transport Service. She stuffed what she needed into a carpet bag and stored her trunk. She didn't need much, a pot to boil water in, soap to clean the dirt and blood from her skirts, and cologne to mask the smell of death. Anything else, she could beg from the supply wagon, or go without.

The horse General Kearney had ordered for her was a strawberry roan named Jessie. Annie loved Jessie's stubborn strength as well as her gentle nature. Annie groomed Jessie gently on the afternoon of the night that they were to cross yet another strange river.

Every river in Virginia was different. The Rapidan swirled black in the moonlight. Huge fires on the banks guided the columns of soldiers across. Now and then a soldier was swept away by the current. The pack mules were unloaded to swim across. The men who carried the animals' burdens cursed as they slipped on the muddy bank. Annie crossed on Jessie, embarrassed to pass the dripping soldiers shivering by the bonfires.

Morning brought sun as Annie and the men rode through the open countryside down the Orange Turnpike. Birds sang in the hedgerows and bees worked the pink and white blossoms of the orchards along the roadsides. A cavalryman Annie only knew as Jacob rode beside her. "Enjoy this while you can," he said. "Soon comes darkness." At her glance, he shrugged. "I know this country. For my money, the Rebs can keep it."

In less than an hour she understood his threat. She fought to hold Jessie back as the road pitched downward. The mare whinnied in protest at the tug of the bit in her mouth. The road plunged into darkness like the mouth of a well.

The forest was a nightmare. Gnarled trees struggled against the coils of massive vines. Ragged ravines led off the road to disappear behind low, dark hills. "This is the land of the grinning ghosts," Jacob told her. "Otherwise known as the Wilderness."

"You're a lot of help," she told him, trying to smile. "Couldn't you just whistle?"

The columns slowed to a halt at a country crossing. The single house at the clearing belonged to the Chancellor family, giving the crossroads the name of Chancellorsville. The house, red brick with graceful white columns, faced a clearing in the woods where two roads met.

About thirty or forty members of the household stared from the wide porch at the army emerging from the woods. Men and horses and supply wagons continued to surround the house and slave quarters out back. By day's end, fifty thousand Federal soldiers were massed around the brick house, with twenty-two thousand more on the way.

With the march over, the men made camp. Before all the tents were even pitched, the smell of beans baking in the coals and fresh boiled coffee filled the clearing.

May Day dawned with a gray drizzle of rain. When an advance guard marched out, leaving Annie's regiment in camp, she presumed that no battle was expected. She was astonished to hear the gunfire begin in midafternoon. Confused, she listened hard, trying to figure out what was going on. Perhaps the guard had only encountered some Confederate scouts. Only when the earth suddenly trembled from the boom of cannons did she realize the guard had encountered the enemy in force. "What are we doing here?" she cried to an orderly. "With that much firing somebody needs us."

He shook his head. "They say General Hooker has already ordered the advance guard to retreat," he said. "We don't need to go asking for trouble. Chances are it will come."

She glared at him and pulled her pillbox out of the tent. By the time she reached the road, she realized he was right. Stretcher-bearers were running from the shadows of the trees, weaving and dodging to avoid the hail of artillery fire. By twilight the wounded had filled the hospital tent to overflowing. Lights winked from across the clearing where the regimental surgeon was operating under a flaring lamp. The mingled smells of brandy and chloroform hung in the wet night air, making Annie's stomach heave with nausea. No painkiller was ever strong enough for the amputations. Annie's whole body flinched from the screams of the men on that badly lit surgical table.

Even when the tent was quiet except for the rumble of the doctors' voices, ominous sounds came from the dense woods. The woods rustled with danger. Strange birds cried out suddenly, bringing a rise of goosebumps on Annie's arms.

The orderly on duty with Annie was a lanky

boy named Andrew with a thatch of pale unruly hair. He was so shy that when she spoke to him, he blushed darker than his hair. At midnight Andrew brought Annie a steaming cup to drink.

"Hot lemonade," he said. "Drink it and you'll rest."

She thanked him but glanced uneasily at her patients. A man could stir in sleep, starting a fatal flow of blood.

"Drink it," Andrew repeated. His tone reminded her of Belle. "Didn't anybody *ever* tell you to do as you are told?"

She laughed and obeyed. Warmed by the hot drink, she leaned back against a tent pole. She only meant to close her eyes while Andrew watched, but fell into an uneasy sleep. She woke to Union cannons firing steadily into the wooded darkness. The sporadic fighting went on all day.

The clearing itself became a madhouse. Groups of angry Southern prisoners were brought in at bayonet point. Even the wounded were furious at being taken from the fight. They shouted threats and curses at their captors as they were herded into an enclosure.

As Annie helped the postsurgical patients back to their beds, she couldn't look at the stacks of arms and legs piled outside the tent for fear she break down altogether. A young infantryman, his head completely swathed by bandages, leaned against Annie as she led him blindly back to the tent. When she thought he was settled, he suddenly sat up. He groped for the side of the cot and cried out, "I can't see. My God, I'm blind. I can't see."

"You don't know that yet," Annie told him. "Lie down and give yourself a chance." He let her ease him back onto the cot but was quiet for only a moment.

"Listen," he whispered tensely. "Put your hand on the ground. The Rebels are on the run. You can feel the rumble of that whole army running away through the ground under this cot."

Annie patted his shoulder and moved on, hoping he was right. As she passed the bed of an old-timer known as "Codger," he shook his head at her.

"Don't swallow that kid's stuff," he told her quietly. "I heard the Reb prisoners talking. They're not scared. I'd bet good money that General Lee is up to something we aren't going to like."

His face was streaked with dirt and gunpowder, but both of his arms were imprisoned in splints. Annie filled a basin with warm water and lifted a soapy cloth to wash his face.

"Have the generals heard this talk?" she asked him, keeping her voice low.

He winced as the wet cloth touched his scraped cheek. "I guess you don't know much about generals," he told her. "Generals don't listen to

147

prisoners." His grin was wicked as he winked at her. "In fact, Annie, my dear, generals may hear but they don't *listen* to anybody."

Aside from the hospital tents, the main camp was strangely quiet. Stretcher-bearers came and went and now and then a messenger raced by. At noon, the men stacked their weapons to prepare a hot meal. Annie tried to ignore the sounds of battle. The firing seemed steadily closer, as if the enemy were in the woods just south of the camp. Annie caught Codger's eyes. He raised his shoulders, then grunted with pain from his wounded arms.

Although the battle never slackened, the men stacked arms again to cook their meals. "What's going on?" she asked Andrew. "Why are the men at rest with that firing so close?"

Andrew looked at her. "There have been messengers all day. The generals *must* know what they are doing."

Andrew flushed as Codger snorted with derision.

Eighteen
May 2 – 27, 1863

WHEN THE SMOKE began to pour into the hospital tent, the wounded soldiers fell into helpless fits of coughing. Annie dropped her basin and raced to the tent flap. Smoke hid the rising moon, but the shells bursting overhead lit a desperate tangle of men and horses. Officers shouted, trying to rally their troops. White-faced stretcher-bearers emerged from the woods, dodging the wagons and pack mules plunging down the road and across the field.

"I belong out there," Annie wailed to Andrew.

"Not on your own," he told her. "Not without orders."

That he was right was small comfort. At dawn's first light, she rose and dressed. By the time the

3rd Michigan Volunteers were ordered out as skirmishers, Jessie was loaded with extra saddlebags along with the pillbox.

The Southern Army was in complete control. Confederate flags advanced steadily through the smoke. Their guns rained a killing fire on the Union lines, plastering the clearing with exploding shells. With their supply lines disrupted, the Union gunners were running out of ammunition.

Annie's skirmishers were posted to a swampy area at the right of the line. They fought their way down clotted trails filled with wagons, artillery, and stray bands of cavalrymen. There was no air, only smoke, the mingled smoke of battle and the blazing forest. And the smoke bred terror. Soldiers threw down their arms and ran for the rear. Frantic cattle staggered against them, fighting to escape from the thick growth of oak trees.

Annie approached the front lines. In her black riding habit, she cantered up to a general conferring with his staff. She carried hardtack and a dozen canteens of coffee as well as her inevitable pillbox.

The Rebel bombardment was at its worst. Three horses of the mounted men in this group were struck with shot as she waited there. When the general tried to send her back to the rear, she held her ground. "I'm not leaving until each of you has something to eat and drink," she told him.

He laughed. "I know when to give up," he told his men. "Take your coffee so we can chase Annie back to safety."

As she left, she rode along the front line. Her colonel saw her and called out to her, "Go back, Annie. The enemy is close. We expect an attack any minute."

She nodded but barely hesitated. She steered Jessie along a line of shallow trenches. When she saw it was filled with men from her division, she smiled down at them. "Boys, do your duty," she called out to them. "Whip the Rebels."

Some of the men partially rose from their cover to cheer her. "Hurrah for Annie!" one cried. Another called out, "Bully for you!"

Their voices revealed their position to the enemy who immediately fired a volley. Annie gasped and reined toward the rear, dodging bullets, knowing she had risked their lives. She galloped Jessie toward the woods and reined her in beside a large oak tree.

Before she could look around, she was pushed roughly aside. A strange Union officer had raced up and shoved his horse between her and the tree to protect himself from the continuing enemy fire. She stared at him in astonishment, unable to believe his cowardice. At that moment a minié ball whizzed by her and struck him. He cried out, groaned, and fell against her, sliding to the ground at Jessie's feet.

The second ball struck before Annie could dismount to help him. This one caught her left hand, its force almost knocking her from Jessie's back. The pain was swift and blazing as the ball glanced off her hand. It shot through her skirt, striking Jessie on the flank.

The mare, panicked by her pain, reared, then bolted. She galloped wildly, running mindlessly into the deep woods. Jessie wound in and out among the trees so rapidly that Annie expected any minute to have her brains dashed out against an overhanging limb. She clung to the mare, talking steadily, as the blood seeped from her own wound to drop in a dark circle on Jessie's mane. She felt her saddlebags being torn away and her bonnet, held only by its loose strings, flying free behind her.

The terrified horse finally charged into a clearing filled with soldiers. Annie gasped with relief to see that she was surrounded by men in blue. "It's that sergeant in petticoats," one of the men cried. "Gentle Annie herself."

As he caught the reins and pulled Jessie to a stop, his companions, men of the 11th Corps, cheered them both.

"What are you doing here?" one of the men asked.

She dismounted, trying to straighten her clothing. "I didn't do it," she told him. "My horse took charge."

"And I guess you're going to tell me that's a horse bite," one of the men said, lifting Annie's bleeding hand.

"It's really nothing, just a graze," she told him, trying to pull it behind her back.

He caught her wrist and called for an orderly. "After all you've done for the rest of us, we can at least spare you a bandage." He insisted she drink a cup of strong coffee, which did help the hammering of her heart. When the wound was dressed, she asked to see General Berry.

"He's not here," the aide said.

"He is too here," she said. "He's my division general and I must see him."

When the aide hesitated, one of the other men spoke up. "Do you think she'd ask to see him if she didn't know him?" he asked. "At least let Berry himself decide."

The aide shrugged and walked away without looking back. From where she stood, Annie saw the aide approach General Berry. The general turned to look at her.

"It's Annie," she heard him say. "Let her come, let her come."

As Annie walked toward him, a prisoner was being delivered to him on the other side. Annie stopped and watched silently as the general spoke to the Confederate officer and accepted his sword.

The general turned and greeted Annie warmly. He asked about her bandaged hand and expressed his dismay that such precious blood should be spilled. "Since you are here," he said, "I have a commission for you. This gentleman at my side is an aide to General Hill. I put this prisoner under your charge. He will walk by your horse to where my men will take responsibility for him."

Annie had never been quite so conscious of the murderous pistols at her belt as she was during that ride. She need not have worried about the man beside her trying to take advantage of her and escape. The officer in gray never raised his eyes to her but walked with stiff-backed dignity into his confinement.

As Annie returned to the hospital to replace her medical supplies, she passed an artillery man lying on the ground outside the tent. He was curled in agony with a deep wound in his side from a bullet that had come out through his shoulder.

She knelt and lifted a canteen to his lips. When he revived a little, she cleaned and bound his wounds. Her own injured hand was a real nuisance. If she had had two good hands she could have pulled him up on Jessie and taken him to the surgeon's tent. The artillery batteries had no surgeons assigned to them. The infantry surgeons, always pressed for time, seldom got to the wounded gunners in time to save them. Annie stayed with the gunner as long as she could, hoping against hope that someone would come along and take pity on him.

The next day's fighting was costly to the leadership of both armies. General Berry, with the old daring he had shown under Kearney, was slain by a Rebel sharpshooter. Word came that the Confederate general "Stonewall" Jackson had been wounded by his own men in a night skirmish. He had survived an amputation but was not expected to live.

Annie was astonished at the sadness in her colonel's voice as he reported Jackson's injury. "Jackson's death might make the Union Army stronger," he told her. "But it would make all mankind poorer. He's not only a brilliant leader but a decent, honorable man."

On orders from General Hooker, who was also injured, the Army of the Potomac withdrew to a new defensive line. The air was thick with smoke from the pine thickets. The raging flames consumed the fallen men and all their equipment. By noon the Confederates were so close that General Lee could be seen in their midst.

That night the soldiers took shelter in the woods or crouched in wet trenches. The river was rising toward flood and only the pontoon bridges across the United States Ford could take them to safety. All rations were gone. The supply trains were on the other side of the river.

By the time this nightmare retreat was over, Stonewall Jackson was dead. He had been mourned all over the Confederacy and buried with high honor in Lexington, Virginia.

The battle at Chancellorsville had cost more than seventeen thousand casualties. This included men who had given up and deserted, as well as those who had died quietly in that flaming wilderness forest.

For all her enduring passion to see her country united again and strong, Annie was exhausted at heart. She had silently grieved for too many fallen young men in gray as well as blue. When "Stonewall" Jackson's last simple words were quoted to her, she wept for him, too, her heart echoing his words. He only wanted "to cross the river and rest under the shade of the trees."

The hospital established near the Potomac Creek bridge quickly filled with the wounded who had been brought out in ambulances and those retrieved later during a temporary truce. Annie slipped quietly back into the hospital and camp routine by day. By night she did not do so well. Her dreams were haunted by what Jacob had called "the land of the grinning ghosts." The phantoms in her dreams didn't grin. The sound

156

of a rifle shot brought her upright. The smoke of evening campfires brought back the crackling of that pine forest trapping the wounded. Sometimes she wakened to find her eyes streaming. "Smoke," she told herself stubbornly. "The tears come from smoke, not grief."

Back at camp, the drills, inspections, reviews, and parades fused together in Annie's mind, until one morning that stood out from all the others.

On May twenty-seventh, General Birney's division was paraded to witness the presentation of the Kearney medals. When the speech making was over, the entire division stood at attention as General Birney handed Annie this award, "For noble sacrifice and heroic service to the Union Army."

As Annie gripped the bronze Maltese cross, her mind filled with the memory of her first sight of that magnificent general raging into battle on his giant white horse. She saluted the general and her comrades, smiling to hide her tears of mingled pride and sorrow.

Nineteen

June 1863 – November 1864

FOLLOWING THEIR VICTORY at Chancellorsville, the Confederate Army advanced into Northern territory. Annie's army, under their new commander, Major General G. G. Meade, marched north to engage them at Gettysburg, Pennsylvania.

For more than two years the Army of the Potomac had fought only in enemy territory. How different it was to campaign among friendly people! In Pennsylvania the grass was green and the mountains blue. Farm girls waved flags from their gates and villagers set out delicious food for the passing troops. The roads were smooth and level and summer hummed in the air. The moon shone on their unfurled flags as they passed through the tiny village of Gettysburg. The old sense of glory shimmered among the stars as the bands filled the night air with music.

The glory was to last only until the morning.

Through the three-day nightmare that followed, Annie lost all sense of reality. Life was suspended in a world controlled by death.

The first shots were fired early on the morning of July first. By nightfall the moon-silvered fields were littered with the dead and dying. By the end of the second day every house and barn was filled with the wounded. The floors of the field hospitals were so slick with human blood that the surgeons fought to keep their balance. The smoke of battle was dense enough to hide the very sun from view.

Only at the end of the third day did the firing finally lessen. Both Union and Confederate soldiers were stacked like cordwood on the hills, the fields, and in the ravines. The remnant of General Lee's proud army either melted away in retreat or threw down their muskets in surrender.

Summer was gone forever from the once open fields around Gettysburg. In its place was a harvest of death. The muskets of fallen soldiers were stacked in endless rows like corn shucks as far as the eye could see. That next day the rain came, dispersing the lingering smoke.

The Confederate Army had lost twenty-five

thousand men. The wagon train that bore their wounded south stretched more than seventeen miles. Annie, stunned with horror, rode with the troops that followed Lee's retreating army. How could they leave so many thousands of wounded men untended and dead men unburied on those ruined rainswept fields?

But more than the loss at Gettysburg darkened that July of 1863. In order to take Fort Sumter and the city of Charleston, the Union Army and Navy launched a joint assault against Battery Wagner on Morris Island. After the pounding of the navy guns, the infantry advanced to fight for the fort in bloody hand-to-hand combat. The 54th Massachusetts Volunteer Infantry Regiment, led by Colonel Robert Gould Shaw, was among the leading regiments in the assault wave. The 54th, an outstanding Negro regiment, performed with conspicuous bravery. On July eighteenth, Colonel Shaw and his Negro orderly died side-by-side on the parapet. Men of both races were buried in shallow sandy graves outside the fort that was pummeled by a seige that continued into October. The heroism of Colonel Shaw and his 54th Massachusetts Volunteers became legendary.

In the dark weeks after Gettysburg, Annie's regiment, along with much of the Union Army, faced a hard decision. The three-year enlistment (which had originally been for three months) was up. Only a fraction of the men who marched off to Blackburn's Ford with such high hopes still lived to make the choice of staying with the army or leaving it.

The officers pleaded with the men to enlist again. "You are seasoned warriors," they said. "If three fourths of you sign up again, you'll get a thirty-day furlough. You'll return with the same regiment number, your flag, and about seven hundred dollars in bounty money. No one but you can set the example for the newly drafted soldiers."

The homesick men argued bitterly. "I've served three years, done my share." "Let the others have their turn."

Will Hammer decided to sign on again. "I'm not going to ask what you'll do, Annie, because I know."

"Has the army taught you mind reading?" she asked him.

He laughed. "I've seen you finish too many hard jobs to think you'd stop short of the end of this."

He was only half right. She would enlist again, but not just to finish a job she had started. She wanted the war over, the senseless wounding and killing stopped. How could she find peace any- where until the guns were silent?

Will left Detroit begging Annie to come with

him. Knowing she was right not to intrude on the Hammer family, she thanked him but explained that she had made "plans."

Her "plans" had begun as a dream. After Gettysburg she had collapsed again, just as she had after Edwin's death and the loss of General Kearney. One night as she lay helplessly weeping, the nurse who shared her tent came to her cot.

"I've read about you ever since the war began, Annie Etheridge," she said. "About your courage, your unfailing gentleness with the wounded, your selflessness."

"Please, Margaret, no," Annie begged.

"Listen to me," Margaret said crossly. "I had decided to hate you. You sounded too good to be true. Now I understand. I'm here because I wanted to serve, too. But a war is like holding your breath, Annie. Do it too long and you become useless to anyone. We aren't through. The South is still strong. How long have you been at war, Annie?"

"Coming up three years," Annie said.

"With no relief from it?" Margaret asked.

Annie sighed. "I've done different things, the hospitals, the Transport Service."

"I'm guessing you'll enlist again, just as I will. But you *have* to catch your breath, Annie. Take your furlough and get away from all this. Do you have family?"

Annie had hesitated. "Not really," she admitted.

Margaret leaned closer. "Listen to me. Neither do I. Let's take leave together. First a day or two here in Washington in a good hotel, clean sheets, fine food and sleep. Then we'll go to my place on Cape Cod."

"Margaret, I couldn't," Annie protested.

"Listen to me," Margaret repeated. "It's the humblest kind of cottage but it's mine. The gulls swing in over the garden and the beach is thick with shells. Peace!"

"I can't let you do this," Annie cried.

"Then I can't do it either," Margaret said dully. "I'll have to stay in Boston with my dull cousins. A woman alone can't rough it on the beach the way two can. And it wouldn't be a free ride," Margaret added. "We'd share the costs of everything. Don't answer now. Just promise to think on it."

The thought had become a dream and the dream a plan.

The two days in Washington were wonderful, but Cape Cod was unforgettable. Margaret was too humble about her home. Blue morning glories tangled by the door and the garden was mostly cooking herbs that scented the salt air at night.

They watched the sun come up across the breakers. They fed beggar gulls with scraps of

Annie's bread left over from their beach picnics. Margaret's books were swollen from the moist air but still readable. Never before had Annie read away one whole afternoon after another. She cried over Dickens's *David Copperfield* and laughed through Thackeray's *Vanity Fair*. When the tide ebbed, they walked the beach barefooted, frightening the shore birds from their path. The days passed in a dreaming peace.

"I can't thank you enough," Annie told Margaret.

"After the war, you'll come again," Margaret said. Annie held the thought like a golden bubble in her mind.

The national cemetery in Gettysburg was dedicated on November nineteenth with rows of white crosses stretching farther than the clusters of stacked arms.

When Will returned in February, almost twenty-seven thousand of the veterans had signed up. General Grant became Commander-in-Chief of the Union Army in March 1864. Annie was attached to the Fifth Army, her third assignment.

Soon after Will's return, one of the men from the old 2nd Michigan Volunteers sought Annie out. "How's our gentle Annie?" he asked. "You remember me?"

"David," she said, "Company C, out of Battle Creek. How good to see you."

He was tall and lean and richly tanned from the Western Campaign. He took the camp stool she offered and looked suddenly embarrassed, twisting his cap in his hands.

"If you're bringing me bad news, let's talk about the weather," she said.

"Not bad news, just strange. Aren't you great buddies with Frank Thompson from Company F?" he asked.

"Good friends," Annie said. "What's new with him?"

After a moment of silence, his words tumbled out swiftly. "He deserted, absent without leave, back in Lebanon, Kentucky, not long after we went west."

"Deserted!" she cried in disbelief. "I can't believe that, not after all the honorable things he did. He was one of the bravest of the aides in battle. How many times have I seen him plunge right into a hail of bullets to pull out a wounded man? And those dangerous spying missions, passing as both a man and a woman, as a white person and a black!"

David held up his hand. "I know all that as well as you do, but there's more, Annie. Frank didn't desert in battle. He got malaria. You know how sick that makes a man."

"Then he only deserted because he was out of his mind from fever," she said defensively.

"I don't think that was it, Annie," he said

165

quietly. "He was plenty sick all right, so bad that they tried to force him into a regimental hospital for treatment."

"Well, *that's* it," she said firmly. "Frank didn't want to be killed by neglect or bad nursing."

"No, Annie," David said patiently, "The plain truth is that Frank didn't want to be exposed." He flushed a deep red. "Early on I marched with a guy from Flint. He'd known Frank before we enlisted. He said Frank wasn't a man at all. He was a Canadian girl named Sarah Emma Edmonds. He thought it was a capital joke on the army. I figure Frank went AWOL to keep from being found out in that regimental hospital."

Annie was speechless with astonishment and remembering. Frank in Washington four years before, not looking that young but still beardless with the smooth face of a girl. His telling how easy it had been to pass as a woman behind Union lines. His reaction when she had accused him of being gossipy. His expression when he told her of burying the girl in a soldier's uniform after Antietam.

"Cat got your tongue, Annie?" David teased her.

"I've never been so amazed in my life," she admitted. Then she laughed. "And happy, too. Nobody ever liked a secret or a prank better than Frank did. That *was* a capital joke on the army, and all of us." She fell silent. How would *that*

166

story strike the men who said women were useless in war?

"I hope that wherever and whoever Frank is, that he's alive and well and having his usual wonderful time."

"Me, too," David said. "They say that at least four hundred women are fighting in this man's army." He rose, smiling. "But we like the way you do your soldiering best!"

Will came back in love with a girl named Martha. He said she was "sweeter than honey on a hot biscuit."

General Grant led battle after battle. Annie's Fifth fought in "the land of the grinning ghosts" again, then the Bloody Angle, Cold Harbor, Belle Plaine, and Hatcher's Run.

When General Grant ordered Annie to City Point Hospital, she felt she should be sent to Petersburg. But she had been separated from her men before. She lent her horse Jessie to a medical aide. "Be good to her," Annie said. "I'll need her in the next campaign."

She didn't dream that Jessie would be cut down by musket fire on the field before Petersburg, or that Hatcher's Run would be the last battle she would take part in.

Twenty

March – April 1865

CITY POINT was near the joining of the James
River with the Appomattox. Established to support Grant's campaign against Petersburg, it was
a bigger supply base than either White House or
Harrison's Landing. Once a village, it had become
a bustling port with wharves and mountains of
supplies. A handsome old mansion looked down
on clusters of pine trees and a tent hospital that
seemed to stretch forever across the mud flats.
By the time Annie arrived, the base boasted a
hotel, barbershops, and even a church.

Grant's siege of Petersburg sent a steady stream
of wounded men into the City Point hospital.
For once there were nurses enough to give the

168

men decent care. Annie loved the young nurses in training but stepped carefully around the Regular Army nurses. Even Dorothea Dix, founder of the Army Nurse Corps, came. She was impressive but as plain and unadorned as she required her nurses to be.

Annie had often feared that her heart might turn to stone from all the horrors she saw. It didn't. The agony of the wounded from Petersburg broke her heart again daily.

The months crawled by as the siege of Petersburg dragged on. But at least the conditions were acceptable. A rail line from Petersburg ran right into the hospital grounds, easing the transport of the wounded. Water was pumped from the river. Cornelia Hancock was there, running a kitchen to provide food for two or three hundred men.

Annie wished she had kept track of the letters she had written for soldiers. There had to be hundreds. She had written so few for herself that she seldom even went to mail call, knowing the orderly would have nothing for her.

When the mail orderly handed her a folded, soiled letter, she looked up at him. "Are you sure it's for me?" she asked.

He nodded. "It says your name right there."

It did indeed. Then she read the date on the letter. "Why, this was written a *long* time ago," she said. "More than a year. It's dated January the fourteenth, 1864."

"It was found on Lieutenant Strachan's body, on the battlefield. It took a while to catch up with you."

She opened it and read the opening words silently to herself, *Annie, dearest friend: I am not long for this world and I wish to thank you for your kindness ere I go.*

The orderly was watching her. "Thank you very much," Annie told him. "You and whoever else got this to me."

She walked beyond the tents to a quiet pine thicket. Finding a mossy stone, she sat in the shadow of a tree. Just reading the words brought back that horrible night in Chancellorsville. She could almost hear the whining shells and smell the smoke of the burning forest:

You were the only one who was ever kind to me since I entered the army. At Chancellorsville, I was shot through the body, the ball entering my side and coming out through the shoulder. I was also hit in the arm and was carried to the hospital in the woods where I lay for hours and not a surgeon would touch me; when you came along and gave me water, and bound up my wounds. I do not know what regiment you belong to, and I don't know if this will ever reach you. There is only one man in your division that I know. I will try and send this to him; his name is Strachan, orderly sergeant in the 63rd Pennsylvania Volunteers.

But should you get this, please accept my heartfelt gratitude; and may God bless you and protect you from all dangers; may you be eminently successful in your present pursuit. I enclose a flower, a present from a sainted mother; it is the only gift I have to send to you. Had I a picture, I would send you one; but I never had but two, one my sister has and the other, the sergeant I told you of; he would give it to you if it is your desire. I know nothing of your history, but I hope you always have and always may be happy; and since I will be unable to see you in this world, I hope I may meet you in that better world where there is no war. May God bless you, both now and forever, is the wish of your grateful friend,

George H. Hill
Cleveland, Ohio

Annie buried her head in her hands, sick despair settling over her. She didn't *need* a picture of George H. Hill. She saw his face, twisted with pain and gentle with gratitude. So many faces, so many lives.

Cornelia Hancock spoke quietly above her. "Annie? Is thee all right?" she asked. "Can I help thee?"

Annie took the hand Cornelia offered and rose to her feet. "Thank you, Cornelia," she said. "You already have."

That night Cornelia's gentle Quaker words

echoed in Annie's head. "Can I help thee?" George Hill's own words were the answer. "A better world, where there is no war."

The weather turned bitter with winter. Snow sifted through the masts of the ships. Christmas brought word that General Sherman had taken Savannah, Georgia. The siege of Petersburg continued. City Point became steadily more crowded. Along with patients and Confederate prisoners, local people sought refuge from the guns of the armies.

Only days after President Lincoln was inaugurated in early March, he came to City Point with his wife and young son, Tad. As before, seeing him made Annie's heart ache. He wore what looked like the same black frock coat and stovepipe hat. He visited every hospital tent, stopping by every bed. Annie, remembering how she had primped for her first view of him, tried to smooth her worn black skirt. He looked older and sadder, but his eyes were as gentle as before.

He even visited the ward of Confederate patients. A female nursing student assigned to that ward joined Annie's table at dinner. The girl shook her head with amazement. "I can't believe President Lincoln," she said with hushed wonder. "He spoke softly and touched each of our patients gently. He was as kind to the enemy wounded as to our own."

An older nurse looked at the girl a moment. "They were *all* his own in the beginning," she reminded her.

Almost at once General Grant left with his army for the May campaign. The bright flags flew and music thrilled as the army poured out of City Point. Annie watched them go wistfully, thinking of the battles she had marched off to.

Overnight, City Point was deserted except for the medical staff, the bull pen of prisoners, and the refugees.

"This place is a ghost town," an orderly teased Annie as their footsteps echoed on the deserted street.

City Point *was* a ghost town, but one haunted by the restless spirit of a giant. President Lincoln was everywhere at all hours. He visited the wounded, often with young Tad. He conferred late with his officers and constantly popped in where the telegraph operators were receiving a steady stream of reports from the front.

Time hung over the base like the May mists on the river. Annie watched dawns come and nights fall without feeling that real days were passing.

"So what's happening?" her patients asked.

She gave them what news she had. "Mrs. Lincoln is going back to Washington," she reported on April first.

"She isn't taking the boy, is she?" one man asked. Annie shook her head. Everybody at City Point liked Tad Lincoln.

The next day the telegrapher burst from his tent to run through the settlement shouting, "We did it. Petersburg is fallen. Petersburg is ours." Annie leaned against a tent pole dizzy with disbelief. Petersburg fallen? After all those long months? It was too wonderful to be true. Only the shouts along the tent rows made the news real.

"That's it," one of the patients told Annie. "There's only that Confederate capital at Richmond left."

The Confederate capital at Richmond fell on the third.

Still Annie held a corner of her heart apart, not accepting the dream. Even when President Lincoln visited the burning Confederate capital and returned to Washington, Annie held herself stiff inside. The speed with which all these things had taken place was too numbing. Only when General Lee signed the papers of surrender at Appomattox on April ninth, did Annie let herself believe. Over. The killing and the maiming were finally over. This seemed a dream too long deferred to be believed.

City Point exploded with celebration. A giant bonfire licked the sky and scattered red lights on the surface of the river. The cheers and shouts of celebration drowned out even the crackling of the flames. The wounded tried to struggle to their feet to share the triumph they had helped win. Nurses and orderlies whirled and danced in the sticky mud of the open corridors between the endless rows of tents.

Annie had always heard of people weeping for joy. She had forgotten how to weep except in grief. But her heart thundered in her chest as she watched the flames rise to challenge the light of the winking stars. She hugged herself tight for fear her heart might leap out of her chest with joy.

City Point became a different place, a festive place. It was almost as if a sweet, healthy wind had blown into that tent city. Even the most severely wounded patients wakened smiling. They chattered all day about home and family, children they hadn't seen, what their plans were, and the very first thing they were going to have to eat when they got out of there.

What possible cloud could dim such complete happiness, so richly earned?

The answer came in a telegraph message from Washington on April fourteenth.

President Lincoln had been shot at Ford's Theatre.

No one believed the message. Patients, order-lies, nurses, and doctors crowded the headquarters of the Quartermaster Department. "It's got to be a rumor," they protested. "They have to be wrong. He cannot die."

"But he held my hand," a patient cried out, showing Annie his palm. "Right here, like this, only a week or so ago, he held my hand."

Annie retreated from her own life into theirs. She refused to let herself think. Instead, she moved like a puppet through the tents, trying to calm the grief-stricken patients, deal with their anger, talk them into waiting until they knew more of what had happened.

The men confined to their cots were frantic. "Go find out what's going on," they begged. "Get us the news."

As she walked out into the open air, she looked toward the crowded harbor. The world opened into darkness under her feet. The flags of all the ships were being lowered to half mast, moving down tortuously, painfully, with the anguished slowness of a funeral march. The President was dead.

Where could she hide from her grief? What had ever been as painful as facing those men? When she stepped inside the tent, the men read her face and turned away in silence.

Within hours black ribbons fluttered grief at every tent flap. Those who could find cloth, made funeral bands to wear around their arms. Annie took out the tiny sewing scissors Sophie had sent her so long before. Helplessly weeping, she sat on the edge of her cot and cut one of her worn riding habits into wide black armbands. She handed them, damp with her own tears, to her mourning patients.

Twenty-one
May 24 – 25, 1865

AFTER THE PELTING RAIN and driving winds and crashing thunder that had plagued the Army of the Potomac through four years of battle, the sun shone on the Union Army's last review.

It poured from the sky in a glittering brightness, winking on polished bayonets, glowing in the metal throats of band instruments, buttering the cannons with an unheard-of gloss. It transformed that broad stream of marching men into a living blue river, punctuated here and there by the rainbow hues of regimental flags.

The Union Army that had begun with a call for seventy-five thousand men had swelled to so great a number that the review went on for days. Yet this was only the remnant. Six hundred thousand Americans, North and South, had lost their lives in battle or from disease. No regimental flag passed that men had not died to defend. No band played whose trumpeter had not sounded mournful notes over the grave of a friend.

On the day that the Fifth Army marched, Annie's colonel cantered up to her followed by an orderly leading a fine horse. He dismounted at her side.

"Of course you will ride," he told her.

"Please, no," Annie said. "I'll march with the men."

"What would Philip Kearney say to that?" he asked.

Annie smiled. "He would understand."

The sergeant at her side laughed. "Beg your pardon, sir, but she's right. He *would* understand. He liked the way she was always right up there with us soldiers."

The colonel stepped back, smiled down at her and saluted. "Very well, Sergeant Annie, at your pleasure."

Her companion grinned down at her as they took their places in the ranks.

Music was everywhere. From the first Annie had loved the bands and the music. Every song brought its own vivid memory. Marching songs from the "land of the grinning ghosts" and their smiling welcome at Gettysburg. Campfire songs, soft from the half darkness by dwindling fires.

A girl's voice lulling stricken men with songs of home and loved ones on a rocking boat on a muddy river.

Best of all was the song she had recognized with her heart the first time she heard it at the Second Battle of Bull Run. That song set the sunlit air atremble from one end of Pennsylvania Avenue to the other. One regimental band after another played the song that had carried them along country roads and through the darkness of the Wilderness, through mud and storm and blistering heat.

"*Glory, glory, Hallelujah. His truth goes marching on.*"

Annie kept in step automatically. She couldn't really see the scene around her for the memories crowding her mind. They came unbidden — memories she knew she would carry to her own grave — from that first baptism in blood at Blackburn's Ford to the burning of Richmond. Faces stood out, even nameless ones. The yellow-haired Southern soldier staring at the sky above Bull Run, Edwin with his hand tight on hers, plunging her heart into a darkness that had never gone away.

From the first there had been reporters. Annie had tired of them quickly. Although she certainly didn't want them intruding on this special day, she was not sorry when one interrupted her with his pressing questions. These kept her grief from

180

spilling into tears on this day of glory.

"Now what, Annie Etheridge?" he asked, running along beside the marching column. His face was too close to Annie's for comfort. When she didn't reply, he chattered on. He only wanted a comment. He reminded her of her heroic career throughout the war.

"Talk to these marching men," she told him. "Quit trying to make a heroine out of me!"

And she had known too many *genuine* heroes who now slept — General Kearney, General Stonewall Jackson, Edwin Powers, General Richardson, George Hill of Cleveland, Ohio, and towering above them all, gaunt and sad, Abraham Lincoln.

"But our readers care about you," he insisted. "Just let me tell them what you're going to do."

She didn't answer him but marched on. So far away and so many years ago Clara Jenkins had stood with a puzzled frown and asked her, "What do you want, Annie?"

Her answer had to be the same now as it was then. "When it comes along, I'll recognize it."

Until she decided what to do, there would be small pleasures to cherish. She was going home. She would hold both of Sophie's hands, meet Will's Martha, and eat all the Michigan mashed potatoes with golden chicken gravy that she could possibly hold.

The Girl Behind
the Story

HER REAL NAME was Anna B. Etheridge. In this fictionalized biography she is called "Annie" as she was in life. The soldiers who praised her in their journals and the newspaper reporters who recorded her deeds had special nicknames for her. They called her, "Gentle Annie," "Michigan Annie," and "that brave little sergeant in petticoats."

These accounts describe her as a small, trim brunette with an elegant carriage and a remarkably pretty face. She was universally known for fearless courage, devotion to duty, and a becoming modesty and gentleness of nature.

We can establish the details of her enlistment and her four years of service with the Union

Army. She was in the front line of almost every major battle fought by the Army of the Potomac from the first, Blackburn's Ford in 1861, through the last, Petersburg in 1865. The battlefield scenes in this book come from eyewitness accounts, as do the reports of her work in the Hospital Transport Service, and nursing duties in other hospital settings.

What we do not know, and what this writer could not locate from any available source, is a single verifiable account of her childhood. We know that she was born Anna Blair but had acquired the last name of Etheridge before she stepped into the spotlight of history in 1861. Other details are so variously recorded as to be irreconcilable. One can only guess that the same modesty that kept her from thinking herself a heroine endowed her with a gentle discretion about discussing her personal life with others.

From among those contradictory accounts, I chose the circumstances that I felt might logically have produced a girl as appealing and capable as Annie Etheridge.

The important thing is that she *did* live, bringing inspiration and healing comfort to legions of young soldiers in the darkest hours of their lives.

After the war, Annie accepted employment in a government office in Washington and married a war veteran who had lost a leg in battle. Although always hailed as a heroine, Annie never thought of herself as outstanding. She brought to her later life the same diligence, modesty, and smiling charm that had won her the nation's heart in wartime.

The Kearney red diamond patch, which Annie wore with such pride, was adopted by other army units. Such insignia still appear on the shoulders and caps of all American army uniforms.

The rumors about Franklin Flint Thompson were true. He was, indeed, a Canadian girl named Sarah Emma Edmonds. Her autobiography, *Nurse and Spy*, was published in 1865 and became a national best-seller.